DEBT OF BONES

Terry Goodkind

Copyright © Terry Goodkind 1998, 2002

All rights reserved

The right of Terry Goodkind to be identified as the
author of this work has been asserted by him in accordance
with the Copyright, Designs and Patents Act 1988

First published in Great Britain in 2002 by Gollancz

This edition published in Great Britain in 2008 by Gollancz
An imprint of the Orion Publishing Group
Orion House, 5 Upper St Martin's Lane, London WC2H 9EA
An Hachette Livre UK Company

5 7 9 10 8 6

A CIP catalogue record for this book is
available from the British Library

ISBN 978 0 75288 9 818

Typeset by Deltatype Ltd, Birkenhead, Merseyside

Printed and bound in the UK by
CPI Group (UK) Ltd, Croydon, CRO 4YY

The Orion Publishing Group's policy is to use papers that
are natural, renewable and recyclable products and made
from wood grown in sustainable forests. The logging and
manufacturing processes are expected to conform to the
environmental regulations of the country of origin.

www.orionbooks.co.uk

To Danny Baror,
my fierce advocate in faraway lands.

AUTHOR'S INTRODUCTION

Debt of Bones was a priceless opportunity for me, amid the sweep of a series, to write an independent short novel delving into the life of a character I've always wanted to write more about. Many times, while writing about the human themes that are important to me, there is more to the story than I can include in the book I'm working on – stories about past events, or how something came to be. This tale lifts the shroud from one of those past events.

How did the boundaries really come to be? What could have brought about such a cataclysmic event? This is, in part, the untold story of the genesis of the boundaries, and yet, it is far more.

I value writing stories set in places I would like to be and about people I admire. I like to write about characters we recognise from our own lives – people we can readily identify and relate to – and also about the people we would like to know. Above all the characters must come alive for me as I write. They must ring true. In this world, as in ours, an individual, no matter how helpless they believe they are, can sometimes make a choice that will change their world, and not always for the better.

This is such a tale.

I wanted to tell the story of one such individual, Abby, a young woman at the mercy of others, powerless against forces she cannot fully understand, much less control, and above all else, desperate for help.

It's also the story of Zedd as a young man, coming into the height of his power, at the centre of a great struggle for the future not only of his people, but of the world. Life and death are at his command, yet he is impotent in the face of wishes he cannot grant – not only to a woman who needs his help, but to himself. Dangling in the balance is the destiny of a young child. Borne on the winds of treachery comes a woman, bearing a Debt of Bones.

I want readers to ask themselves what they would do if faced with the same choices as Abby and Zedd. How would they choose?

This is not only the story of how the boundaries came to be, but the dawning of the world into which Richard and Kahlan will be born.

– Terry Goodkind

'What do you got in the sack, dearie?'

Abby was watching a distant flock of whistling swans, graceful white specks against the dark soaring walls of the Keep, as they made their interminable journey past ramparts, bastions, towers and bridges lit by the low sun. The sinister spectre of the Keep had seemed to be staring back the whole of the day as Abby had waited. She turned to the hunched old woman in front of her.

'I'm sorry, did you ask me something?'

'I asked what you got in your sack.' As the woman peered up, she licked the tip of her tongue through the slot where a tooth was missing. 'Something precious?'

Abby clutched the burlap sack to herself as she shrank a little from the grinning woman. 'Just some of my things, that's all.'

An officer, trailed by a troop of assistants, aides, and guards, marched out from under the massive portcullis that loomed nearby. Abby and the rest of the supplicants waiting at the head of the stone bridge moved tighter to the side, even though the soldiers had ample room to pass. The officer, his grim gaze unseeing as he swept by, didn't return the salute as the bridge guards clapped fists to the armour over their hearts.

All day, soldiers from different lands, as well as the Home Guard from the vast city of Aydindril below, had been coming and going from the Keep. Some had looked travel-sore. Some wore uniforms still filthy with dirt, soot, and blood from recent battles. Abby had even seen two officers from her homeland of Pendisan Reach. They had looked to her to be little more than boys, but boys with the thin veneer of youth shedding too soon, like a snake casting off its skin before its time, leaving the emerging maturity scarred.

Abby had also seen such an array of important people as she could scarcely believe: sorceresses, councillors, and even a Confessor come up from the Confessor's Palace down in the city. On her way up to the Keep, there was rarely a turn in the winding road that hadn't offered Abby a view of the sprawling splendour in white stone that was the Confessor's Palace. The alliance of the Midlands, headed by the Mother Confessor herself, held council in the palace, and there, too, lived the Confessors.

In her whole life, Abby had seen a Confessor only once before. The woman had come to see Abby's mother and Abby, not ten years at the time, had been unable to keep from staring at the Confessor's long hair. Other than her mother, no woman in Abby's small town of Coney Crossing was sufficiently important to have hair long enough to touch the shoulders. Abby's own fine, dark brown hair covered her ears but no more.

Coming through the city on the way to the Keep, it had been hard for her not to gape at noble women with hair to their shoulders and even a little beyond. But the Confessor going up to the Keep, dressed in the simple, satiny, black dress of a Confessor, had hair that reached halfway down her back.

She wished she could have had a better look at the rare sight of such long luxuriant hair and the woman important enough to possess it, but Abby had gone to a knee with the rest of the company at the bridge, and like the rest of them feared to raise her bowed head to look up lest she meet the gaze of the other. It was said that to meet the gaze of a Confessor could cost you your mind if you were lucky, and your soul if you weren't. Even though Abby's mother had said it was untrue, that only the deliberate touch of such a woman could effect such a deed, Abby feared, this day of all days, to test the stories.

The old woman in front of her, clothed in layered skirts topped with one dyed of henna and mantled with a dark draping shawl, watched the soldiers pass and then leaned closer. 'Do better to bring a bone, dearie. I hear that there be those in the city who will sell a bone such as you need – for the right price. Wizards don't take no salt pork for a need. They got salt pork.' She glanced past Abby to the others to see them occupied with their own interests. 'Better to sell your things and hope you have enough to buy a bone. Wizards don't want what some country girl brung 'em. Favours from wizards don't come easy.' She took a surreptitious glance at the backs of the soldiers as they reached the far side of the bridge. 'Not even for those doing their bidding, it would seem.'

'I just want to talk to them. That's all.'

'Salt pork won't get you a talk, neither, as I hear tell.' She eyed Abby's hand trying to cover the smooth round shape beneath the burlap. 'Or a jug you made. That what it is, dearie?' Her brown eyes, set in a wrinkled leathery mask, turned up, peering with sudden, humourless intent. 'A jug?'

'Yes,' Abby said. 'A jug I made.'

The woman smiled her scepticism and fingered a lick of short grey hair back under her wool head-wrap. Her gnarled fingers closed around the smocking on the forearm of Abby's crimson dress, pulling the arm up a bit to have a look.

'Maybe you could get the price of a proper bone for your bracelet.'

Abby glanced down at the bracelet made of two wires intricately twisted together in interlocking circles. 'My mother gave me this. It has no value but to me.'

A slow smile spread on the woman's weather-cracked lips. 'The spirits believe that there is no stronger power than a mother's want to protect her child.'

Abby gently pulled her arm away. 'The spirits know the truth of that.'

Uncomfortable under the scrutiny of the suddenly talkative woman, Abby looked away, seeking a safe refuge for her gaze. It made her dizzy to look down into the yawning chasm beneath the bridge, and she was weary of watching the Wizard's Keep, so she pretended that her attention had been caught as an excuse to turn back towards the collection of people, mostly men, waiting with her at the head of the bridge. She busied herself with nibbling on the last crust of bread from the loaf she had bought down in the market before coming up to the Keep.

Abby felt awkward talking to strangers. In her whole

life she had never seen so many people, much less people she didn't know. She knew every person in Coney Crossing. The city made her apprehensive, but not as apprehensive as the Keep towering on the mountain above it, and that, not as much as her reason for being there.

She just wanted to go home. But there would be no home, at least nothing to go home to, if she didn't do this.

Their attention drawn by the rattling roar of hooves, all eyes turned toward the gaping portcullis. Huge horses, all dusky brown or black and bigger than any Abby had ever seen, came thundering towards them. Men bedecked with polished breastplates, chain-mail, and leather, and most carrying lances or poles topped with long flags of high office and rank, urged their mounts onward. They raised dust and gravel as they gathered speed crossing the bridge, a wild rush of colour and sparkles of light from metal flashing past. Sanderian lancers, from the descriptions Abby had heard. She had trouble imagining the enemy with the nerve to go up against men such as these.

Her stomach roiled. She realized she had no need to imagine and no reason to put her hope in brave men such as those lancers. Her only hope was the wizard, and that hope was slipping away with the day. There was nothing for it but to wait.

Abby turned back to the Keep just in time to see a statuesque woman in simple robes stride out through the opening in the massive stone wall. Her fair skin stood out all the more against straight dark hair parted in the middle and readily reaching her shoulders. Some of the men had been whispering about the sight of the Sanderian officers, but at the sight of the woman everyone fell to silence. The four soldiers at the head of the stone bridge made way for the woman as she approached the supplicants.

'Sorceress,' the old woman whispered to Abby.

Abby hardly needed the old woman's counsel to know it was a sorceress. Abby was well acquainted with the simple flaxen robes, decorated at the neck with yellow and red beads sewn in the ancient symbols of the profession. Some of her earliest memories were of being held in her mother's arms and touching beads like those she saw now.

The sorceress bowed her head to the people and then offered a smile. 'Please forgive us for keeping you waiting out here the whole of the day. It is not from lack of respect nor something we customarily do, but with the war on our hands such precautions are regrettably unavoidable. We hope none took offence at the delay.'

The crowd mumbled that they didn't. Abby doubted there was one among them bold enough to claim otherwise.

'How goes the war?' a man behind asked.

The sorceress's even gaze turned to him. 'With the blessings of the good spirits, it will end soon.'

'May the spirits will that D'Hara is crushed,' beseeched the man.

Without response, the sorceress appraised the faces watching her, waiting to see if anyone else would speak or ask a question. None did.

'Please, come with me, then. The council meeting has ended, and a couple of the wizards will take the time to see you all.'

As the sorceress started toward the Keep, three men arrived. Their fine clothes made the simple garb of people at the bridge, by comparison, seem almost thread-bare. As the procession shuffled toward the Keep, the three men strode up along the supplicants and put themselves at the head of the line, right in front of the old woman. The oldest of the three, dressed in rich robes of dark purple with contrasting red sewn inside the length of the slits up the sleeves, looked to be a noble with his two advisors, or perhaps guards.

The woman's expression darkened. She snatched a velvet sleeve. 'Who do you think you are,' she snapped, 'taking a place before me, when I've been here the whole of the day?'

He scowled down at the gnarled fingers clutching his sleeve. When his eyes turned up at her, they were filled with menace.

'You don't mind, do you?'

It didn't sound at all to Abby like a question.

The old woman withdrew her hand and fell mute.

The man, the ends of his grey hair coiled on his shoulders, glanced at Abby. His hooded eyes gleamed with challenge. She swallowed and remained silent. She didn't have any objection, either, at least none she was willing to voice. For all she knew, the noble was important enough to see to it that she was denied an audience. She couldn't afford to take the chance now that she was this close.

Abby was distracted by a tingling sensation from the bracelet. Blindly, her fingers glided over the wrist of the hand holding the sack. The wire bracelet felt warm. The last time it had done that was the day her mother had died. In the presence of so much magic as was at a place such as this, it didn't really surprise her. Dust swirled

9

around their feet as the ragged crowd followed behind the sorceress.

'Mean, they are,' the woman whispered over her shoulder. 'Mean as a winter night, and just as cold.'

'Those men?' Abby whispered back.

'No.' The woman tilted her head. 'Sorceresses. Wizards, too. That's who. All those born with the gift of magic. You better have something important in that sack, or the wizards might turn you to dust for no other reason than that they'd enjoy it.'

Abby pulled her sack tight in her arms. The meanest thing her mother had done in the whole of her life was to die before she could see her granddaughter.

Abby swallowed back the urge to cry and prayed to the dear spirits that the old woman was wrong about wizards, and that they were as understanding as sorceresses. She prayed fervently that this wizard would help her. She prayed for forgiveness, too – that the good spirits would understand.

Abby worked at holding a calm countenance even though her insides were in turmoil. She pressed a fist to her stomach. She prayed for strength. Even in this, she prayed for strength.

The sorceress, the three men, the old woman, Abby, and then the rest of the supplicants, passed under the fangs of the huge iron portcullis and onto the Keep grounds. Inside the massive outer wall Abby was surprised to discover the air warm. Outside it had been a chill autumn day, but inside the air was spring-fresh and warm.

The road up the mountain, the stone bridge over the chasm, and then the opening under the portcullis appeared to be the only way into the Keep, unless you were a bird. Soaring walls of dark stone with high windows surrounded the gravel courtyard inside. There were a number of doors around the courtyard, and ahead, a roadway tunnelled deeper into the Keep.

Despite the warm air, Abby was chilled to the bone by the place. She wasn't sure that the old woman wasn't right about wizards. Life in Coney Crossing was far removed from matters of wizards.

Abby had never seen a wizard before, nor did she know anyone who had, except for her mother, and her mother never spoke of them except to caution that where wizards were concerned, you couldn't trust even what you saw with your own eyes.

The sorceress led them up four granite steps worn smooth over the ages by countless footsteps, through a doorway set back under a lintel of pink-flecked black granite, and into the Keep proper. The sorceress lifted an arm into the darkness, sweeping it to the side. Lamps along the wall sprang to flame.

It had been simple magic – not a very impressive display of the gift – but several of the people behind fell to worried whispering as they passed on through the wide hall. It occurred to Abby that if this little bit of conjuring would frighten them, then they had no business going to see wizards.

They wended their way across the sunken floor of an imposing anteroom the likes of which Abby could never even have imagined. Red marble columns all around supported arches below balconies. In the centre of the room a fountain sprayed water high overhead. The water fell back to cascade down through a succession of ever larger scalloped bowls. Officers, sorceresses, and a variety of others sat about on white marble benches or huddled in small groups, all engaged in seemingly earnest conversation masked by the sound of water.

In a much smaller room beyond, the sorceress gestured for them to be seated at a line of carved oak benches along one wall. Abby was bone-weary and relieved to sit at last.

Light from windows above the benches lit three tapestries hanging on the high far wall. The three together covered nearly the entire wall and made up one scene of a grand procession through a city. Abby had never seen anything like it, but with the way her dreads careened through her thoughts, she could summon little pleasure in seeing even such a majestic tableau.

In the centre of the cream-coloured marble floor, inset in brass lines, was a circle with a square inside it, its corners touching the circle. Inside the square sat another circle just large enough to touch the insides of the square. The centre circle held an eight-pointed star. Lines radiated out from the points of the star, piercing all the way through both circles, every other line bisecting a corner of the square.

The design, called a Grace, was often drawn by those with the gift. The outer circle represented the beginnings of the infinity of the spirit world out beyond. The square represented the boundary separating the spirit world – the underworld, the world of the dead – from the inner circle, which represented the limits of the world of life. In the centre of it all was the star, representing the Light – the Creator.

It was a depiction of the continuum of the gift: from the Creator, through life, and at death crossing the boundary to eternity with the spirits in the Keeper's realm

of the underworld. But it represented a hope, too – a hope to remain in the Creator's Light from birth, through life, and beyond, in the underworld.

It was said that only the spirits of those who did great wickedness in life would be denied the Creator's Light in the underworld. Abby knew she would be condemned to an eternity with the Keeper of darkness in the underworld. She had no choice.

Her posture erect, the sorceress folded her hands in a careful, elegant manner, as if the very act was an essential part of an elaborate spell. 'An aide will come to get you each in turn. A wizard will see each of you. The war burns hot; please keep your petition brief.' Her calm gaze glided down the line of seated people. 'It is out of a sincere obligation to those we serve that the wizards see supplicants, but please try to understand that individual desires are often detrimental to the greater good. By pausing to help one, then many are denied help. Thus, denial of a request is not a denial of your need, but acceptance of greater need. In times of peace it is rare for wizards to grant the narrow wants of supplicants. At a time like this, a time of a great war, it is almost unheard of. Please understand that it has not to do with what we would wish, but is a matter of necessity.'

She watched the line of supplicants, but saw none willing to abandon their purpose. Abby certainly would not.

'Very well then. We have two wizards able to take supplicants at this time. We will bring you each to one of them.'

The sorceress turned to leave. Alarmed to find her only chance suddenly slipping away, Abby rose to her feet.

'Please, mistress, a word if I may?'

The sorceress turned an unsettling gaze on Abby. 'Speak.'

Gathering up her courage along with her burlap sack, Abby stepped forward. She had to swallow before she could bring herself to say the words.

'I must see the First Wizard himself. Wizard Zorander.'

One eyebrow arched. 'The First Wizard is a very busy man.'

Fearing her chance would slip away, Abby thrust a hand into her sack and pulled out the neck band from her mother's robes. She stepped into the centre of the Grace and reverently kissed the familiar red and yellow beads on the neck band.

'I am Abigail, born of Helsa. On the Grace and my mother's soul, I must see Wizard Zorander. Please. It is no trivial journey I have made. Lives are at stake.'

The sorceress watched the beaded band being returned to the sack. 'Abigail, born of Helsa.' Her gaze rose to meet Abby's. 'I will take your words to the First Wizard.'

'Mistress.' Abby turned to see the old woman on her feet. 'I would be well pleased to see the First Wizard, too.'

The three men rose up. The oldest, the one apparently in charge of the three, gave the sorceress a look so barren of timidity that it bordered on contempt. His long grey hair fell forward over his velvet robes as he glanced down the line of seated people, seeming to dare them to stand. When none did, he returned his attention to the sorceress.

'I will see Wizard Zorander.'

The sorceress appraised those on their feet and then looked down the line of supplicants on the bench. 'The

First Wizard has earned a name: the wind of death. He is feared no less by many of us than by our enemies. Anyone else who would bait fate?'

None of those on the bench had the courage to gaze into her fierce, sorceress eyes. To the last they all silently shook their heads. 'Please wait,' she said to those seated. 'Someone will shortly be out to take you to a wizard.' She looked once more to the five people standing. 'Are you all very, very sure of this?'

Abby nodded. The old woman nodded. The noble glared.

'Very well then. Come with me.'

The noble and his two men stepped in front of Abby. The old woman seemed content to take a station at the end of the line. They were led deeper into the Keep, through narrow halls and wide corridors, some dark and austere and some of astounding grandeur. Everywhere there were soldiers of the Home Guard, their breastplates or chain-mail covered with red tunics banded around their edges in black. All were heavily armed with swords or battle-axes, all had knives, and many additionally carried pikes tipped with winged and barbed steel.

At the top of a broad white marble stairway the stone railings spiralled at the ends to open wide onto a room of warm oak panelling. Several of the raised panels held lamps with polished silver reflectors. Atop a three-legged table sat a double-bowl cut-glass lamp with twin chimneys, their flames adding to the mellow light from the reflector lamps. A thick carpet of ornate blue patterns covered nearly the entire wood floor.

To each side of a double door stood one of the meticulously dressed Home Guard. Both men were equally huge. They looked to be men more than able to handle any trouble that might come up the stairs.

The sorceress nodded towards the dozen thickly tufted leather chairs set in four groups. Abby waited until the others had seated themselves in two of the groupings and then sat by herself in another. She placed the sack in her lap and rested her hands over its contents.

The sorceress stiffened her back. 'I will tell the First Wizard that he has supplicants who wish to see him.'

A guard opened one of the double doors for her. As she was swallowed into the great room beyond, Abby was able to snatch a quick glimpse. She could see that it was well lighted by glassed skylights. There were other doors in the grey stone of the walls. Before the door closed, Abby was also able to see a number of people, men and women both, all rushing hither and yon.

Abby sat turned away from the old woman and the three men as with one hand she idly stroked the sack in her lap. She had little fear that the men would talk to her, but she didn't want to talk to the woman; it was a distraction. She passed the time going over in her mind what she planned to say to Wizard Zorander.

At least she tried to go over it in her mind. Mostly, all she could think about was what the sorceress had said, that the First Wizard was called the wind of death, not only by the D'Harans, but also by his own people of the Midlands. Abby knew it was no tale to scare off supplicants from a busy man. Abby herself had heard people whisper of their great wizard, 'the wind of death'. Those whispered words were uttered in dread.

The lands of D'Hara had sound reason to fear this man as their enemy; he had laid waste to countless of their army, from what Abby had heard. Of course if they hadn't invaded the Midlands, bent on conquest, they would not have felt the hot wind of death.

Had they not invaded, Abby wouldn't be sitting there in the Wizard's Keep – she would be at home, and everyone she loved would be safe.

Abby marked again the odd tingling sensation from the bracelet. She ran her fingers over it, testing its unusual warmth. This close to a person of such power it didn't surprise her that the bracelet was warming. Her mother had told her to wear it always, and that someday it would be of value. Abby didn't know how, and her mother had died without ever explaining.

Sorceresses were known for the way they kept secrets, even from their own daughters. Perhaps if Abby had been born gifted . . .

She sneaked a peek over her shoulder at the others. The old woman was leaning back in her chair, staring at the doors. The noble's attendants sat with their hands folded as they casually eyed the room.

The noble was doing the oddest thing. He had a lock of sandy-coloured hair wound around a finger. He stroked his thumb over the lock of hair as he glared at the doors.

Abby wanted the wizard to hurry up and see her, but time stubbornly dragged by. In a way, she wished he would refuse. No, she told herself, that was unacceptable. No matter her fear, no matter her revulsion, she must do this. Abruptly, the door opened. The sorceress strode out towards Abby.

The noble surged to his feet. 'I will see him first.' His voice was cold threat. 'That is not a request.'

'It is our right to see him first,' Abby said without

forethought. When the sorceress folded her hands, Abby decided she had best go on. 'I've waited since dawn. This woman was the only one waiting before me. These men came at the last of the day.'

Abby started when the old woman's gnarled fingers gripped her forearm. 'Why don't we let these men go first, dearie? It matters not who arrived first, but who has the most important business.'

Abby wanted to scream that her business was important, but she realized that the old woman might be saving her from serious trouble in accomplishing her business. Reluctantly, she gave the sorceress a nod. As the sorceress led the three men through the door, Abby could feel the old woman's eyes on her back. Abby hugged the sack against the burning anxiety in her abdomen and told herself that it wouldn't be long, and then she would see him.

As they waited, the old woman remained silent, and Abby was glad for that. Occasionally, she glanced at the door, imploring the good spirits to help her. But she realized it was futile; the good spirits wouldn't be disposed to help her in this.

An abrupt, shrill, shrieking roar came from the room beyond the heavy doors. The awful sound, like metal being ripped apart, hurt Abby's ears. It ended with a resonant boom accompanied by a blinding flash of light flaring out from all around the doors. They shuddered on their hinges. The lamps rattled.

Sudden silence rang in Abby's ears. She found herself gripping the arms of the chair.

Both doors opened. The noble's two attendants

marched out, followed by the sorceress. The three stopped in the waiting room. Abby sucked a breath.

One of the two men was cradling the noble's head in the crook of an arm. The wan features of the face were frozen in a mute scream. Thick strings of blood dripped onto the carpet.

'Show them out,' the sorceress hissed through gritted teeth to one of the two guards at the door.

The guard dipped his pike towards the stairs, ordering them ahead, and then followed the two men down. Crimson drops splattered onto the white marble of the steps as they descended. Abby sat in stiff, wide-eyed shock.

The sorceress wheeled back to Abby and the old woman.

The woman rose to her feet. 'I believe that I would rather not bother the First Wizard today. I will return another day, if need be.'

She hunched lower towards Abby. 'I am called Mariska.' Her brow drew down. 'May the good spirits grant that you succeed.'

She shuffled to the stairs, rested a hand on the marble railing, and started down. The sorceress snapped her fingers and gestured. The remaining guard rushed to accompany the woman, as the sorceress turned back to Abby.

'The First Wizard will see you now.'

Abby gulped air, trying to get her breath as she staggered to her feet.

'What happened? Why did the First Wizard do that?'

'The man was sent on behalf of another to ask a

question of the First Wizard. The First Wizard gave his answer.'

Abby clutched her sack to herself for dear life as she gaped at the blood on the floor. 'Might that be the answer to my question, if I ask it?'

'I don't know the question you would ask.' For the first time, the sorceress's expression softened just a bit. 'Would you like me to see you out? You could see another wizard or, perhaps, after you've given more thought to your petition, return another day, if you still wish it.'

Abby fought back tears of desperation. There was no choice. She shook her head. 'I must see him.'

The sorceress let out a deep breath. 'Very well.' She put a hand under Abby's arm as if to keep her on her feet. 'The First Wizard will see you now.'

Abby hugged the contents of her sack as she was led into the chamber where waited the First Wizard. Torches in iron sconces were not yet burning. The late afternoon light from the glassed roof windows was still strong enough to illuminate the room. It smelled of pitch, lamp oil, roasted meat, wet stone, and stale sweat.

Inside, confusion and commotion reigned. There were people everywhere, and they all seemed to be talking at once. Stout tables set about the room in no discernible pattern were covered with books, scrolls, maps, chalk, unlit oil lamps, burning candles, partially eaten meals, sealing wax, pens, and a clutter of every sort of odd object, from balls of knotted string to half-spilled sacks of sand. People stood about the tables, engaged in conversations or arguments as others tapped passages in books, pored over scrolls, or moved little painted weights about on maps. Others rolled slices of roasted meat plucked from platters and nibbled as they watched or offered opinions between swallows.

The sorceress, still holding Abby under her arm, leaned closer as they proceeded. 'You will have the First Wizard's divided attention. There will be other people talking to him at the same time. Don't be distracted. He will be listening to you as he also listens to or talks to others. Just ignore the others who are speaking and ask what you have come to ask. He will hear you.'

Abby was dumbfounded. 'While he's talking to other people?'

'Yes.' Abby felt the hand squeeze her arm ever so slightly. 'Try to be calm, and not to judge by what has come before you.'

The killing. That was what she meant. That a man had come to speak to the First Wizard, and he had been killed for it. She was simply supposed to put that from her thoughts? When she glanced down, she saw that she was walking through a trail of blood. She didn't see the headless body anywhere.

Her bracelet tingled so that she looked down at it. The hand under her arm halted her. When Abby looked up, she saw a confusing knot of people before her. Some rushed in from the sides as others rushed away. Some flailed their arms as they spoke with great conviction. So many were talking that Abby could scarcely understand a word of it. At the same time, others were leaning in, nearly whispering. She felt as if she were confronting a human beehive.

Abby's attention was snagged by a form in white to the side. The instant she saw the long fall of hair and the violet eyes looking right at her, Abby went rigid. A small cry escaped her throat as she fell to her knees and bowed over until her back protested. She trembled and shuddered, fearing the worst.

In the instant before she dropped to her knees, she had seen that the elegant, satiny, white dress was cut square at the neck, the same as the black dresses had been. The long flag of hair was unmistakable. Abby had never seen the woman before, but without doubt knew who she was. There could be no mistaking this woman. Only one of them wore the white dress.

It was the Mother Confessor herself.

She heard muttering above her, but feared to listen, lest it was death being summoned.

'Rise, my child,' came a clear voice.

Abby recognized it as the formal response of the Mother Confessor to one of her people. It took a moment for Abby to realize it represented no threat, but simple acknowledgement. She stared at a smear of blood on the floor as she debated what to do next. Her mother had never instructed her as to how to conduct herself should she ever meet the Mother Confessor. As far as she knew, no one from Coney Crossing had ever seen the Mother Confessor, much less met her. Then again, none of them had ever seen a wizard, either.

Overhead, the sorceress whispered a growl. 'Rise.'

Abby scurried to her feet, but kept her eyes to the floor, even though the smear of blood was making her sick. She could smell it, like a fresh butchering of one of their animals. From the long trail, it looked as if the body had been dragged away to one of the doors in the back of the room.

The sorceress spoke calmly into the chaos. 'Wizard

Zorander, this is Abigail, born of Helsa. She wishes a word with you. Abigail, this is First Wizard Zeddicus Zu'l Zorander.'

Abby dared to cautiously lift her gaze. Hazel eyes gazed back.

To each side before her were knots of people: big, forbidding officers – some of them looked as if they might be generals; several old men in robes, some simple and some ornate; several middle-aged men, some in robes and some in livery; three women – sorceresses all; a variety of other men and women; and the Mother Confessor.

The man at the centre of the turmoil, the man with the hazel eyes, was not what Abby had been expecting. She had expected some grizzled, gruff old man. This man was young – perhaps as young as she. Lean but sinewy, he wore the simplest of robes, hardly better made than Abby's burlap sack – the mark of his high office.

Abby had not anticipated this sort of man in such an office as that of First Wizard. She remembered what her mother had told her – not to trust what your eyes told you where wizards were concerned.

All about, people spoke to him, argued at him, a few even shouted, but the wizard was silent as he looked into her eyes. His face was pleasing enough to look upon, gentle in appearance, even though his wavy brown hair looked ungovernable, but his eyes . . . Abby had never seen the likes of those eyes. They seemed to see all, to know all, to understand all. At the same time they were bloodshot and weary-looking, as if sleep eluded him. They had, too, the slightest glaze of distress. Even so, he was calm at the centre of the storm. For that moment that his attention was on her, it was as if no one else were in the room.

The lock of hair Abby had seen around the noble's finger was now held wrapped around the First Wizard's finger. He brushed it to his lips before lowering his arm.

'I am told you are the daughter of a sorceress.' His voice was placid water flowing through the tumult raging all about. 'Are you gifted, child?'

'No, sir . . .'

Even as she answered, he was turning to another who had just finished speaking. 'I told you, if you do, we chance losing them. Send word that I want him to cut south.'

The tall officer to whom the wizard spoke threw his hands up. 'But he said they've reliable scouting information that the D'Harans went east on him.'

'That's not the point,' the wizard said. 'I want that pass to the south sealed. That's where their main force went; they have gifted among them. They are the ones we must kill.'

The tall officer was saluting with a fist to his heart as the wizard turned to an old sorceress. 'Yes, that's right, three invocations before attempting the transposition. I found the reference last night.'

The old sorceress departed to be replaced by a man jabbering in a foreign tongue as he opened a scroll and held it up for the wizard to see. The wizard squinted towards it, reading a moment before waving the man away, while giving orders in the same foreign language.

The wizard turned to Abby. 'You're a skip?'

Abby felt her face heat and her ears burn. 'Yes, Wizard Zorander.'

'Nothing to be ashamed of, child,' he said while the Mother Confessor herself was whispering confidentially in his ear.

But it *was* something to be ashamed of. The gift hadn't passed onto her from her mother – it had skipped her.

The people of Coney Crossing had depended on Abby's mother. She helped with those who were ill or hurt. She advised people on matters of community and those of family. For some she arranged marriages. For some she meted out discipline. For some she bestowed favours available only through magic. She was a sorceress; she protected the people of Coney Crossing.

She was revered openly. By some, she was feared and loathed privately.

She was revered for the good she did for the people of Coney Crossing. By some, she had been feared and loathed because she had the gift – because she wielded magic. Others wanted nothing so much as to live their lives without any magic about.

Abby had no magic and couldn't help with illness or injury or shapeless fears. She dearly wished she could, but she couldn't. When Abby had asked her mother why she would abide all the thankless resentment, her mother told her that helping was its own reward and you should not expect gratitude for it. She said that if you went through life expecting gratitude for the help you provided, you might end up leading a miserable life.

When her mother was alive, Abby had been shunned in subtle ways; after her mother died, the shunning became more overt. It had been expected by the people of Coney Crossing that she would serve as her mother had served. People didn't understand about the gift, how it often wasn't passed onto an offspring; instead they thought Abby selfish.

The wizard was explaining something to a sorceress about the casting of a spell. When he finished, his gaze swept past Abby on its way to someone else. She needed his help, now.

'What is it you wanted to ask me, Abigail?'

Abby's fingers tightened on the sack. 'It's about my home of Coney Crossing.' She paused while the wizard pointed in a book being held out to him. He rolled his hand at her, gesturing for her to go on as a man was explaining an intricacy to do with inverting a duplex spell. 'There's terrible trouble there,' Abby said. 'D'Haran troops came through the Crossing . . .'

The First Wizard turned to an older man with a long white beard. By his simple robes, Abby guessed him as a wizard, too.

'I'm telling you, Thomas, it can be done,' Wizard Zorander insisted. 'I'm not saying I agree with the council, I'm just telling you what I found and their unanimous decision that it be done. I'm not claiming to understand the details of just how it works, but I've studied it; it can be done. As I told the council, I can activate it. I have yet to decide if I agree with them that I should.'

The man, Thomas, wiped a hand across his face. 'You mean what I heard is true, then? That you really do think it's possible? Are you out of your mind, Zorander?'

'I found it in a book in the First Wizard's private enclave. A book from before the war with the Old World. I've seen it with my own eyes. I've cast a whole series of verification webs to test it.' He turned his attention to

Abby. 'Yes, that would be Anargo's legion. Coney Crossing is in Pendisan Reach.'

'That's right,' Abby said. 'And so then this D'Haran army swept through there and—'

'Pendisan Reach refused to join with the rest of the Midlands under central command to resist the invasion from D'Hara. Standing by their sovereignty, they chose to fight the enemy in their own way. They have to live with the consequences of their actions.'

The old man was tugging on his beard. 'Still, do you know if it's real? All proven out? I mean, that book would have to be thousands of years old. It might have been conjecture. Verification webs don't always confirm the entire structure of such a thing.'

'I know that as well as you, Thomas, but I'm telling you, it's real,' Wizard Zorander said. His voice lowered to a whisper. 'The spirits preserve us, it's genuine.'

Abby's heart was pounding. She wanted to tell him her story, but she couldn't seem to get a word in. He had to help her. It was the only way.

An army officer rushed in from one of the back doors. He pushed his way into the crowd around the First Wizard.

'Wizard Zorander! I've just got word! When we unleashed the horns you sent, they worked! Urdland's force turned tail!'

Several voices fell silent. Others didn't.

'At least three thousand years old,' the First Wizard said to the man with the beard. He put a hand on the newly-arrived officer's shoulder and leaned close. 'Tell General Brainard to hold short at the Kern River. Don't burn the bridges, but hold them. Tell him to split his men. Leave half to keep Urdland's force from changing their mind; hopefully they won't be able to replace their field wizard. Have Brainard take the rest of his men north to help cut Anargo's escape route; that's where our concern lies, but we may still need the bridges to go after Urdland.'

One of the other officers, an older man looking possibly to be a general himself, went red in the face. 'Halt at the river? When the horns have done their job, and we have them on the run? But why? We can take them down before they have a chance to regroup and join up with another force to come back at us!'

Hazel eyes turned towards the man. 'And do you know what waits over the border? How many men will die if Panis Rahl has something waiting that the horns can't turn away? How many innocent lives has it already cost us? How many of our men will die to bleed them on their own land – land we don't know as they do?'

'And how many of our people will die if we don't eliminate their ability to come back at us another day? We must pursue them. Panis Rahl will never rest. He'll be working to conjure up something else to gut us all in our sleep. We must hunt them down and kill every last one!'

'I'm working on that,' the First Wizard said cryptically.

The old man twisted his beard and made a sarcastic face. 'Yes, he thinks he can unleash the underworld itself on them.'

Several officers, two of the sorceresses, and a couple of the men in robes paused to stare in open disbelief.

The sorceress who had brought Abby to the audience leaned close. 'You wanted to talk to the First Wizard. Talk. If you have lost your nerve, then I will see you out.'

Abby wet her lips. She didn't know how she could talk into the middle of such a roundabout conversation, but she knew she must, so she just started back in.

'Sir, I don't know anything about what my homeland of Pendisan Reach has done. I know little of the king. I don't know anything about the council, or the war, or any of it. I'm from a small place, and I only know that the people there are in grave trouble. Our defenders were overrun by the enemy. There is an army of Midlands men who drive towards the D'Harans.'

She felt foolish talking to a man who was carrying on a half-dozen conversations all at once. Mostly, though, she felt anger and frustration. Those people were going to die if she couldn't convince him to help.

'How many D'Harans?' the wizard asked.

Abby opened her mouth, but an officer spoke in her place. 'We're not sure how many are left in Anargo's legion. They may be wounded, but they're an enraged wounded bull. Now they're in sight of their homeland. They can only come back at us, or escape us. We've got Sanderson sweeping down from the north and Mardale cutting up from the southwest. Anargo made a mistake going into the Crossing; in there he must fight us or run for home. We have to finish them. This may be our only chance.'

The First Wizard drew a finger and thumb down his smooth jaw. 'Still, we aren't sure of their numbers. The scouts were dependable, but they never returned. We can only assume they're dead. And why would Anargo do such a thing?'

'Well,' the officer said, 'it's the shortest escape route back to D'Hara.'

The First Wizard turned to a sorceress to answer a question she had just finished. 'I can't see how we can afford it. Tell them I said no. I'll not cast that kind of web for them and I'll not give them the means to it for no more offered than a "maybe".'

The sorceress nodded before rushing off.

Abby knew that a web was the spell cast by a sorceress. Apparently the spell cast by a wizard was called the same.

'Well, if such a thing is possible,' the bearded man was saying, 'then I'd like to see your exegesis of the text. A three-thousand-year-old book is a lot of risk. We've no clue as to how the wizards of that time could do most of what they did.'

The First Wizard, for the first time, cast a hot glare towards the man. 'Thomas, do you want to see exactly what I'm talking about? The spell-form?'

Some of the people had fallen silent at the tone in his voice. The First Wizard threw open his arms, urging everyone back out of his way. The Mother Confessor stayed close behind his left shoulder. The sorceress beside Abby pulled her back a step.

The First Wizard motioned. A man snatched a small sack off the table and handed it to him. Abby noticed that some of the sand on the tables wasn't simply spilled, but had been used to draw symbols. Abby's mother had occasionally drawn spells with sand, but mostly used a variety of other things, from ground bone to dried herbs. Abby's mother had used sand for practice; spells, real spells, had to be drawn in proper order and without error.

The First Wizard squatted down and took a handful of sand from the sack. He drew on the floor by letting the sand drizzle from the side of his fist.

Wizard Zorander's hand moved with practised precision. His arm swept around, drawing a circle. He returned for a handful of sand and drew an inner circle. It appeared he was drawing a Grace.

Abby's mother had always drawn the square second; everything in order inward and then the rays back out. Wizard Zorander drew the eight-pointed star inside the smaller circle. He drew the lines radiating outward, through both circles, but left one absent.

He had yet to draw the square, representing the boundary between worlds. He was the First Wizard, so Abby guessed that it wasn't improper to do it in a different order than a sorceress in a little place like Coney Crossing. But several of the men Abby took as wizards, and the two sorceresses behind him, were turning grave glances to one another.

Wizard Zorander laid down the lines of sand for two sides of the square. He scooped up more sand from the sack and began the last two sides.

Instead of a straight line, he drew an arc that dipped well into the edge of the inner circle – the one representing the world of life. The arc, instead of ending at the outer circle, crossed it. He drew the last side, likewise arced, so that it too crossed into the inner circle. He brought the line to meet the other where the ray from the Light was missing. Unlike the other three points of the square, this last point ended outside the larger circle – in the world of the dead.

People gasped. A hush fell over the room for a moment before worried whispers spread among those gifted.

Wizard Zorander rose. 'Satisfied, Thomas?'

Thomas's face had gone as white as his beard. 'The

Creator preserve us.' His eyes turned to Wizard Zorander. 'The council doesn't truly understand this. It would be madness to unleash it.'

Wizard Zorander ignored him and turned towards Abby. 'How many D'Harans did you see?'

'Three years past, the locust swarms came. The hills of the Crossing were brown with them. I think I saw more D'Harans than I saw locusts.'

Wizard Zorander grunted his discontent. He looked down at the Grace he had drawn. 'Panis Rahl won't give up. How long, Thomas? How long until he finds something new to conjure and sends Anargo back on us?' His gaze swept among the people around him. 'How many years have we thought we would be annihilated by the invading horde from D'Hara? How many of our people have been killed by Rahl's magic? How many thousands have died of the fevers he sent? How many thousands have blistered and bled to death from the touch of the shadow people he conjured? How many villages, towns, and cities has he wiped from existence?'

When no one spoke, Wizard Zorander went on.

'It has taken us years to come back from the brink. The war has finally turned; the enemy is running. We now have three choices. The first choice is to let him run for home and hope he never comes back to again visit us with his brutality. I think it would only be a matter of time until he tried again. That leaves two realistic options. We can either pursue him into his lair and kill him for good at the cost of tens, perhaps hundreds of thousands of our men – or I can end it.'

Those gifted among the crowd cast uneasy glances to the Grace drawn on the floor.

'We still have other magic,' another wizard said. 'We can use it to the same effect without unleashing such a cataclysm.'

'Wizard Zorander is right,' another said, 'and so is the council. The enemy has earned this fate. We must set it upon them.'

The room fell again to arguing. As it did, Wizard Zorander looked into Abby's eyes. It was a clear instruction to finish her supplication.

'My people – the people in Coney Crossing – have been taken by the D'Harans. They have others, too, who they've captured. They have a sorceress holding the captives with a spell. Please, Wizard Zorander, you must help me.

'When I was hiding, I heard the sorceress talking to their officers. The D'Harans plan to use the captives as shields. They will use the captives to blunt the deadly magic you send against them, or to blunt the spears and arrows the Midlands army sends against them. If they decide to turn and attack, they plan to drive the captives ahead. They called it "dulling the enemies' weapons on their own women and children".'

No one looked at her. They were all once again engaged in their mass talking and arguing. It was as if the lives of all those people were beneath their consideration.

Tears stung at Abby's eyes. 'Either way all those innocent people will die. Please, Wizard Zorander, we must have your help, otherwise they'll all die.'

He looked her way briefly. 'There is nothing we can do for them.'

Abby panted, trying to hold back the tears. 'My father was captured, along with others of my kin. My husband is among the captives. My daughter is among them. She is not yet five. If you send magic, they will be killed. If you attack, they will be killed. You must rescue them, or hold the attack.'

He looked genuinely saddened. 'I'm sorry. I can't help them. May the good spirits watch over them and take their souls to the Light.' He began turning away.

'No!' Abby screamed. Some of the people fell silent. Others only glanced her way as they went on. 'My child! You can't!' She thrust a hand into the sack. 'I have a bone—'

'Doesn't everyone?' he grumbled, cutting her off. 'I can't help you.'

'But you must!'

'We would have to abandon our cause. We must take the D'Haran force down – one way or another. Innocent though those people are, they are in the way. I can't allow the D'Harans to succeed in such a scheme or it would encourage its widespread use, and then even more innocents would die. The enemy must be shown that it will not deter us from our course.'

'NO!' Abby wailed. 'She's only a child! You're condemning my baby to death! There are other children! What kind of monster are you?'

No one but the wizard was even listening to her any more as they all went on with their talking.

The First Wizard's voice cut through the din and fell on her ears as clearly as the knell of death. 'I am a man who must make choices such as this one. I must deny your petition.'

Abby screamed with the agony of failure. She wasn't even to be allowed to show him.

'But it's a debt!' she cried. 'A solemn debt!'

'And it cannot be paid now.'

Abby screamed hysterically. The sorceress began pulling her away. Abby broke from the woman and ran out of the room. She staggered down the stone steps, unable to see through the tears.

At the bottom of the steps she buckled to the floor in helpless sobbing. He wouldn't help her. He wouldn't help a helpless child. Her daughter was going to die.

Abby, convulsing in sobs, felt a hand on her shoulder. Gentle arms pulled her closer. Tender fingers brushed back her hair as she wept into a woman's lap. Another person's hand touched her back and she felt the warm comfort of magic seeping into her.

'He's killing my daughter,' she cried. 'I hate him.'

'It's all right, Abigail,' the voice above said. 'It's all right to weep for such a pain as this.'

Abby wiped at her eyes, but couldn't stop the tears. The sorceress was there, beside her, at the bottom of the steps.

Abby looked up at the woman in whose consoling arms she lay. It was the Mother Confessor herself. But any sense of wonderment was swamped in a sea of despair, and any sense of caution was suddenly pointless. The woman could do her worst, for all Abby cared. What did it matter, what did any of it matter, now?

'He's a monster,' she sobbed. 'He is truly named. He is the ill wind of death. This time it's my baby he's killing, not the enemy.'

'I understand why you feel that way, Abigail,' the Mother Confessor said, 'but it is not true.'

'How can you say that? My daughter has not yet had a chance to live, and he will kill her! My husband will die. My father, too, but he has had a chance to live a life. My baby hasn't!'

She fell to hysterical wailing again, and the Mother Confessor once again drew her into comforting arms. Comfort was not what Abby wanted.

'You have just the one child?' the sorceress asked.

Abby nodded as she sucked a breath. 'I had another, a boy, but he died at birth. The midwife said I will have no more. My little Jana is all I will ever have.' The wild agony of it ripped through her. 'And he will kill her. Just as he killed that man before me. Wizard Zorander is a monster. May the good spirits strike him dead!'

With a poignant expression, the sorceress smoothed Abby's hair back from her forehead. 'You don't understand. You see only a part of it. You don't mean what you say.'

But she did. 'If you had—'

'Delora understands,' the Mother Confessor said, gesturing towards the sorceress. 'She had a daughter of ten years, and a son, too.'

Abby peered up at the sorceress. She gave Abby a sympathetic smile and a nod to confirm the truth of it.

'I, too, have a daughter,' the Mother Confessor said. 'She is twelve. Delora and I both understand your pain. So does the First Wizard.'

Abby's fists tightened. 'He couldn't! He's hardly more than a boy himself, and he wants to kill my baby. He is the wind of death and that's all he cares about – killing people!'

The Mother Confessor patted the stone step beside

her. 'Abigail, sit up here beside me. Let me tell you about the man in there.'

Still weeping, Abby pushed herself up and slid on to the step. The Mother Confessor was older by maybe twelve or fourteen years, and pleasant-looking, with those violet eyes. Her mass of long hair reached her waist. She had a warm smile. It had never occurred to Abby to think of a Confessor as a woman, but that was what she saw now. She didn't fear this woman as she had before; nothing she did could be worse than what already had been done.

'I sometimes minded Zeddicus when he was but a toddler and I was still coming into womanhood.' The Mother Confessor gazed off with a wistful smile. 'I swatted his bottom when he misbehaved, and later twisted his ear to make him sit at a lesson. He was mischief on two legs, driven not by guile but by curiosity. He grew into a fine man.

'For a long time, when the war with D'Hara started, Wizard Zorander wouldn't help us. He didn't want to fight, to hurt people. But in the end, when Panis Rahl, the leader of D'Hara, started using magic to slaughter our people, Zedd knew that the only hope to save more lives in the end was to fight.

'Zeddicus Zu'l Zorander may look young to you, as he did to many of us, but he is a special wizard, born of a wizard and a sorceress. Zedd was a prodigy. Even those other wizards in there, some of them his teachers, don't always understand how he is able to unravel some of the enigmas in the books or how he uses his gift to bring so much power to bear, but we do understand that he has heart. He uses his heart, as well as his head. He was named First Wizard for all these things and more.'

'Yes,' Abby said, 'he is very talented at being the wind of death.'

The Mother Confessor smiled a small smile. She tapped her chest. 'Among ourselves, those of us who really know him call him the trickster. The trickster is the name he has truly earned. We named him the wind of death for others to hear, so as to strike terror into the hearts of the enemy. Some people on our side take that name to heart. Perhaps, since your mother was gifted, you can understand how people sometimes unreasonably fear those with magic?'

'And sometimes,' Abby argued, 'those with magic really are monsters who care nothing for the life they destroy.'

The Mother Confessor appraised Abby's eyes a moment, and then held up a cautionary finger. 'In confidence, I am going to tell you about Zeddicus Zu'l Zorander. If you ever repeat this story, I will never forgive you for betraying my confidence.'

'I won't, but I don't see—'

'Just listen.'

After she seemed sure Abby would remain silent, the Mother Confessor began. 'Zedd married Erilyn. She was a wonderful woman. We all loved her very much, but not as much as did he. They had a daughter.'

Abby's curiosity got the best of her. 'How old is she?'

'About the age of your daughter,' Delora said.

Abby swallowed at the measured irony of the sorceress's words. 'I see.'

'When Zedd became First Wizard, things were grim.' Desolate reflection haunted the Mother Confessor's violet eyes. 'Panis Rahl had conjured the shadow people.'

'Shadow people . . . ? I'm from Coney Crossing, I've never heard of such a thing.'

'Well, the war had been bad enough, but then Panis Rahl taught his wizards to conjure shadow people.' The Mother Confessor sighed at the anguish of retelling the story. 'They are so called because they are like shadows in the air. They have no precise shape or form. They are not living, but created out of magic. Weapons have no more effect on them than they would have on smoke.

'You can't hide from the shadow people. They drift towards you across fields, or through the woods. They find you.

'When they touch someone, the person's whole body blisters and swells until their flesh splits open. They die in screaming agony. Not even the gift can heal one touched by a shadow person.

'As the enemy attacked, their wizards would send the shadow people out ahead. In the beginning whole battalions of our brave young soldiers were found killed to a man. We saw no hope. It was our darkest hour.'

'And Wizard Zorander was able to stop them?' Abby asked.

The Mother Confessor nodded. 'He studied the problem and then conjured battle horns. Their magic swept the shadow people away like smoke in the wind. The magic coming from the horns also traced its way back through the spell, to seek out the one who cast it, and kill them. The horns aren't foolproof, though, and Zedd must constantly alter their magic to keep up with the way the enemy changes their conjuring.

'Panis Rahl summoned other magic, too: fevers and sickness, wasting illnesses, fogs that caused blindness – all sorts of horrors. Zedd worked day and night, and managed to counter them all. While Panis Rahl's magic was being checked, our troops were once again able to fight on even terms. Because of Wizard Zorander, the tide of battle turned.'

'Well, that much of it is good, but—'

The Mother Confessor again lifted her finger, commanding silence. Abby held her tongue as the woman lowered her hand and went on.

'Panis Rahl was enraged at what Zedd had done. He tried and failed to kill him, so he instead sent a quad to kill Erilyn.'

'A quad? What's a quad?'

'A quad,' the sorceress answered, 'is a unit of four special assassins sent with the protection of a spell from the one who sent them: Panis Rahl. It is not only their assignment to kill the victim, but to make it unimaginably torturous and brutal.'

Abby swallowed. 'And did they . . . murder his wife?'

The Mother Confessor leaned closer. 'Worse. They left her, her legs and arms all broken, to be found still alive.'

'Alive?' Abby whispered. 'Why would they leave her alive, if it was their mission to kill her?'

'So that Zedd would find her all broken and bleeding and in inconceivable agony. She was able only to whisper his name in love.' The Mother Confessor leaned even closer. Abby could feel the breath of the woman's whispered words against her own face. 'When he used his gift to try to heal her, it activated the worm spell.'

Abby had to force herself to blink. 'Worm spell . . . ?'

'No wizard would have been able to detect it.' The

Mother Confessor clawed her fingers and, in front of Abby's stomach, spread her hands outward, in a tearing gesture. 'The spell ripped her insides apart. Because he had used his loving touch of magic, she died in screaming pain as he knelt helpless beside her.'

Wincing, Abby touched her own stomach, almost feeling the wound. 'That's terrible.'

The Mother Confessor's violet eyes held an iron look. 'The quad also took their daughter. Their daughter, who had seen everything those men had done to her mother.'

Abby felt tears burning her eyes again. 'They did that to his daughter, too?'

'No,' the Mother Confessor said. 'They hold her captive.'

'Then she still lives? There is still hope?'

The Mother Confessor's satiny white dress rustled softly as she leaned back against the white marble balustrade and nested her hands in her lap. 'Zedd went after the quad. He found them, but his daughter had been given to others, and they passed her onto yet others, and so on, so they had no idea who had her, or where she might be.'

Abby looked to the sorceress and back to the Mother Confessor. 'What did Wizard Zorander do to the quad?'

'No less than I myself would have done.' The Mother Confessor's face had taken on a mask of cold rage. Her tone was even more chilling than the words themselves. 'He made them regret ever being born. For a very long time he made them regret it.'

Abby shrank back. 'I see.'

As the Mother Confessor drew a calming breath, the sorceress took up the story. 'As we speak, Wizard

45

Zorander uses a spell that none of us understands; it holds Panis Rahl at his palace in D'Hara. It helps blunt the magic Rahl is able to conjure against us, and enables our men to drive his troops back whence they came.

'But Panis Rahl is consumed with wrath for the man who has thwarted his conquest of the Midlands. Hardly a week passes that an attempt is not made on Wizard Zorander's life. Rahl sends dangerous and vile people of all sorts. Even the Mord-Sith.'

Abby's breath caught. That was a word she had heard. With guarded interest, she ventured a question. 'What are Mord-Sith?'

The sorceress smoothed back her glossy black hair as she glared with a venomous expression. 'Mord-Sith are women who, along with their red leather uniform, wear a single long braid as the mark of their profession. They are trained in the torture and killing of those with the gift. If a gifted person tries to use their magic against a Mord-Sith, she is able to capture their magic and use it against them. There is no escaping a Mord-Sith.'

'But surely, a person as strong in the gift as Wizard Zorander—'

'Even he would be lost if he tried to use magic against a Mord-Sith,' the Mother Confessor said. 'A Mord-Sith can be defeated with common weapons – but not with magic. Only the magic of a Confessor works against them. I have killed two.

'In part because of the brutal nature of the training of Mord-Sith, they have been outlawed for as long as anyone knows, but in D'Hara the ghastly tradition of taking young women to be indoctrinated as Mord-Sith continues to this day. D'Hara is a distant and secretive land. We don't know much about it, except what we have learned through unfortunate experience.

'Mord-Sith have captured several of our wizards and sorceresses. Once captured, they cannot kill themselves, nor can they escape. Before they die, they give over everything they know. Panis Rahl knows of our plans.

'We, too, have managed to get our hands on several high-ranking D'Harans, and through the touch of Confessors, we know the extent of how we have been compromised. Time works against us.'

Abby wiped the palms of her hands on her thighs. 'And that man who was killed just before I went in to see the First Wizard, he couldn't have been an assassin; the two with him were allowed to leave.'

'No, he was not an assassin.' The Mother Confessor folded her hands. 'I believe Panis Rahl knows of the spell Wizard Zorander discovered, that it has the potential to obliterate all of D'Hara. Panis Rahl is desperate to rid himself of Wizard Zorander.'

The Mother Confessor's violet eyes, always revealing keen intellect, now glistened with the hidden weight of untold terrible knowledge. Abby couldn't bear the scrutiny of those eyes, and looked away. She picked at a stray thread on her sack. 'But I don't see what this has to do with denying me help to save my daughter. He has a daughter. Wouldn't he do anything to get her back? Wouldn't he do whatever he must to have his daughter back and safe?'

The Mother Confessor's head lowered and she stroked her fingers over her brow, as if trying to rub at a grievous ache. 'The man who came before you was a messenger. His message had been passed through many hands so that it could not be traced back to its source.'

Abby felt cold goose bumps running up her arms. 'What was the message?'

'The lock of hair he brought was from Zedd's daughter. Panis Rahl offered the life of Zedd's daughter if Zedd would surrender himself to Panis Rahl to be executed.'

Abby clutched at her sack. 'But wouldn't a father who loved his daughter do even this to save her life?'

'At what cost?' the Mother Confessor whispered. 'At the cost of the lives of all those who will die without his help?

'He couldn't do such a selfish thing, even to save the life of one he loves more than any other. Before he denied your daughter help, he had just refused the offer, thus sentencing his own innocent daughter to death.'

Abby felt her hopes again tumbling into blackness. The thought of Jana's terror, of her being hurt, made Abby dizzy and sick. Tears began running down her cheeks again.

'But I'm not asking him to sacrifice everyone else to save her.'

The sorceress gently touched Abby's shoulder. 'He believes that sparing those people harm would mean letting the D'Harans escape to kill more people in the end.'

Abby snatched desperately for a solution. 'But I have a bone.'

The sorceress sighed. 'Abigail, half the people who come to see a wizard bring a bone. Hucksters convince

48

supplicants that they are true bones. Desperate people, just like you, buy them.'

'Most of them come seeking a wizard to somehow give them a life free of magic,' the Mother Confessor said. 'Most people fear magic, but I'm afraid that with the way it's been used by D'Hara, they now want nothing so much as to never again see magic. An ironic reason to buy a bone, and doubly ironic that they buy sham bones, thinking they have magic, in order to petition to be free of magic.'

Abby blinked. 'But I bought no bone. This is a debt true. On my mother's deathbed she told me of it. She said it was Wizard Zorander himself bound in it.'

The sorceress squinted her scepticism. 'Abigail, true debts of this nature are exceedingly rare. Perhaps it was a bone she had and you only thought . . .'

Abby held her sack open for the sorceress to see. The sorceress glanced in and fell silent. The Mother Confessor looked in the sack for herself.

'I know what my mother told me,' Abby insisted. 'She also told me that if there was any doubt, he had but to test it, then he would know it true, for the debt was passed down to him from his father.'

The sorceress stroked the beads at her throat. 'He could test it. If it is true, he would know. Still, solemn debt though it may be, that doesn't mean that the debt must be paid now.'

Abby leaned boldly towards the sorceress. 'My mother said it is a debt true, and that it had to be paid. Please, Delora, you know the nature of such things. I was so confused when I met with him, with all those people shouting. I foolishly failed to press my case by asking that he test it.' She turned and clutched the Mother Confessor's arm. 'Please, help me? Tell him what I have and ask that he test it?'

The Mother Confessor considered behind a blank expression. At last she spoke. 'This involves a debt bound in magic. Such a thing must be considered seriously. I will speak to Wizard Zorander on your behalf and request that you be given a private audience.'

Abby squeezed her eyes shut as tears sprang anew. 'Thank you.' She put her face in both hands and began to weep with relief at the flame of hope rekindled.

The Mother Confessor gripped Abby's shoulders. 'I said I will try. He may deny my request.'

The sorceress snorted a humourless laugh. 'Not likely. I will twist his ear, too. But Abigail, that does not mean that we can convince him to help you – bone or no bone.'

Abby wiped her cheek. 'I understand. Thank you both. Thank you both for understanding.'

With a thumb, the sorceress wiped a tear from Abby's chin. 'It is said that the daughter of a sorceress is a daughter to all sorceresses.'

The Mother Confessor stood and smoothed her white dress. 'Delora, perhaps you could take Abigail to a rooming house for women travellers. She should get some rest. Do you have money, child?'

'Yes, Mother Confessor.'

'Good. Delora will take you to a room for the night. Return to the Keep just before sunrise. We will meet you and let you know if we were able to convince Zedd to test your bone.'

'I will pray to the good spirits that Wizard Zorander will see me and help my daughter.' Abby felt sudden shame at her own words. 'And I will pray, too, for his daughter.'

The Mother Confessor cupped Abby's cheek. 'Pray for all of us, child. Pray that Wizard Zorander unleashes the magic against D'Hara, before it is too late for all the children of the Midlands – old and young alike.'

On their walk down to the city, Delora kept the conversation from Abby's worries and hopes, and what magic might contribute to either. In some ways, talking with the sorceress was reminiscent of talking with her mother. Sorceresses evaded talk of magic with one not gifted, daughter or not. Abby got the feeling that it was as uncomfortable for them as it was for Abby when Jana asked how a mother came to have a child in her tummy.

Even though it was late, the streets were teeming with people. Worried gossip of the war floated to Abby's ears from every direction. At one corner a knot of women murmured tearfully of menfolk gone for months with no word of their fate.

Delora took Abby down a market street and had her buy a small loaf of bread with meats and olives baked right inside. Abby wasn't really hungry. The sorceress made her promise that she would eat. Not wanting to do anything to cause disfavour, Abby promised.

The rooming house was up a side-street among tightly packed buildings. The racket of the market carried up the narrow street and flittered around buildings and through tiny courtyards with the ease of a chickadee through a dense wood. Abby wondered how people could stand to live so close together and with nothing to see but other houses and people. She wondered, too, how she was going to be able to sleep with all the strange sounds and noise, but then, sleep had rarely come since she had left home, despite the dead-quiet nights in the countryside.

The sorceress bid Abby a good night, putting her in the hands of a sullen-looking woman of few words who led her to a room at the end of a long hall and left her to her night's rest, after collecting a silver coin. Abby sat on the edge of the bed and, by the light of a single lamp sitting on a shelf by the bed, eyed the small room as she nibbled at the loaf of bread. The meat inside was tough and stringy, but had an agreeable flavour, spiced with salt and garlic.

Without a window, the room wasn't as noisy as Abby had feared it might be. The door had no bolt, but the woman who kept the house had said in a mumble for her not to fret, that no men were allowed in the establishment. Abby set the bread aside and, at a basin atop a simple stand two strides across the room, washed her face. She was surprised at how dirty it left the water.

She twisted the lever stem on the lamp, lowering the wick as far as it would go without snuffing the flame; she didn't like sleeping in the dark in a strange place. Lying in bed, staring up at the water-stained ceiling, she prayed earnestly to the good spirits, despite knowing that they would ignore a request such as she made. She closed her eyes and prayed for Wizard Zorander's daughter, too. Her prayers were fragmented by intruding fears that felt as if they clawed her insides raw.

She didn't know how long she had lain in the bed, wishing for sleep to take her, wishing for morning to come, when the door slowly squeaked open. A shadow climbed the far wall.

Abby froze, eyes wide, breath held tight, as she watched a crouched figure move towards the bed. It wasn't the woman of the house. She would be taller. Abby's fingers tightened on the scratchy blanket, thinking that maybe she could throw it over the intruder and then run for the door.

'Don't be alarmed, dearie. I've just come to see if you had success up at the Keep.'

Abby gulped air and sat up in the bed. 'Mariska?' It was the old woman who had waited with her in the line all day. 'You frightened the wits out of me!'

The small flame from the lamp reflected in a sharp shimmer in the woman's eye as she surveyed Abby's face. 'Worse things to fear than your own safety.'

'What do you mean?'

Mariska smiled. It was not a reassuring smile. 'Did you get what you wanted?'

'I saw the First Wizard, if that's what you mean.'

'And what did he say, dearie?'

Abby swung her feet down off the bed. 'That's my business.'

The sly smile widened. 'Oh, no, dearie, it's our business.'

'What do you mean by that?'

'Answer the question. You've not much time left. Your family has not much time left.'

Abby shot to her feet. 'How do you—'

The old woman seized Abby's wrist and twisted until Abby was forced to sit. 'What say the First Wizard?'

'He said he couldn't help me. Please, that hurts. Let me go.'

'Oh, dearie, that's too bad, it is. Too bad for your little Jana.'

'How . . . how do you know about her? I never—'

'So, Wizard Zorander denied your petition. Such sad news.' She clicked her tongue. 'Poor, unfortunate, little Jana. You were warned. You knew the price of failure.'

She released Abby's wrist and turned away. Abby's mind raced in hot panic as the woman shuffled towards the door.

'No! Please! I'm to see him again, tomorrow. At sunrise.'

Mariska peered back over her shoulder. 'Why? Why would he agree to see you again, after he has denied you? Lying will buy your daughter no more time. It will buy her nothing.'

'It's true. I swear it on my mother's soul. I talked to the sorceress, the one who took us in. I talked to her and the Mother Confessor, after Wizard Zorander denied my petition. They agreed to convince him to give me a private audience.'

Her brow bunched. 'Why would they do this?'

Abby pointed to her sack sitting on the end of the bed. 'I showed them what I brought.'

With one gnarled finger, Mariska lifted the burlap. She peered inside, considering for a moment what she saw in the sack, before finally gliding closer to Abby.

'You have yet to show this to Wizard Zorander?'

'That's right. They will get me an audience with him. I'm sure of it. Tomorrow, he will see me.'

From her bulky waistband, Mariska drew a knife. She waved it slowly back and forth before Abby's face. 'We grow weary of waiting for you.'

Abby licked her lips. 'But I—'

'In the morning I leave for Coney Crossing. I leave to see your frightened little Jana.' Her hand slid behind Abby's neck. Fingers like oak roots gripped Abby's hair, holding her head fast. 'If you bring him right behind me, she will go free, as you were promised.'

Abby couldn't nod. 'I will. I swear. I'll convince him. He is bound by a debt.'

Mariska put the point of the knife so close to Abby's eye that it brushed her eyelashes. Abby feared to blink.

'Arrive late, and I will stab my knife in little Jana's eye. Stab it through. I will leave her the other so that she can watch as I cut out her father's heart, just so that she will know how much it will hurt when I do her. Do you understand, dearie?'

Abby could only whine that she did, as tears streamed down her cheeks.

'There's a good girl,' Mariska whispered from so close that Abby was forced to breathe the spicy stink of the woman's sausage dinner. 'If we even suspect any tricks, they will all die.'

'No tricks. I'll hurry. I'll bring him.'

Mariska kissed Abby's forehead. 'You're a good mother.' She released Abby's hair. 'Jana loves you. She cries for you day and night.'

After Mariska closed the door, Abby curled into a trembling ball in the bed and wept against her knuckles.

Delora leaned closer as they marched across the broad rampart. 'Are you sure you're all right, Abigail?'

Wind snatched at her hair, flicking it across her face. Brushing it from her eyes, Abby looked out at the sprawl of the city below beginning to coalesce out of the gloom. She had been saying a silent prayer to her mother's spirit.

'Yes. I just had a bad night. I couldn't sleep.'

The Mother Confessor's shoulder pressed against Abby's from the other side. 'We understand. At least he agreed to see you. Take heart in that. He's a good man, he really is.'

'Thank you,' Abby whispered in shame. 'Thank you both for helping me.'

The people waiting along the rampart – wizards, sorceresses, officers, and others – all momentarily fell silent and bowed towards the Mother Confessor as the three women passed. Among several people she recognized from the day before, Abby saw the wizard Thomas, grumbling to himself and looking hugely impatient and vexed as he shuffled through a handful of papers covered in what Abby recognized as magical symbols.

At the far end of the rampart they came to the stone face of a round turret. The eyebrow where the soffit met the edge of a steep, slate tile roof protruded out over a low, round-topped door. The sorceress rapped her knuckles briefly, then lifted the lever and opened the heavy oak door without bothering to wait for a reply. She caught the twitch of Abby's brow.

'He rarely hears the knock,' she explained in a hushed tone.

The secluded room held a wealth of treasures. Shelves were crammed tight here and there with jars, jugs, and colored glass vessels holding what Abby imagined had to be strange substances. A variety of small, ornate boxes sitting in corners and up high hid from view what had to be secrets. Weighty books stacked everywhere hinted at

obscure knowledge. The spines of the books were gilded not only with rich designs, but words in exotic languages. Corner cases with glassed doors held some of the tomes, along with a few oddly shaped items embellished with strange designs.

The finely-fit stone of the walls and heavy oak beams imparted a cozy feel. A round window to Abby's right overlooked the city below and another on the opposite wall looked up at the soaring walls of the Keep. The highest walls in the distance glowed pink in the first faint rays of dawn. An elaborate iron candelabrum held a small army of candles that provided a warm glow to the room.

Wizard Zorander, his unruly wavy brown hair hanging down around his face as he stood leaning on his hands, was absorbed in studying a book lying open before him. The magnificent desk, its top polished to a mirror finish, was banded all around with ornate carving. More pronounced carvings on a heavy, straight-back oak chair behind the wizard glistened in the candlelight. On a chest to the side sat a pewter mug and a plate littered with the remains of a long-finished meal.

'Wizard Zorander,' the sorceress announced, 'we bring Abigail, born of Helsa.'

'Bags, woman,' the wizard grouched without looking up, 'I heard your knock, as I always do.'

'Don't you curse at me, Zeddicus Zu'l Zorander,' Delora grumbled back.

He ignored the sorceress, rubbing his smooth chin as he considered the book before him. 'Welcome, Abigail.'

Abby's fingers fumbled at the sack. But then she remembered herself and curtsied. 'Thank you for seeing me, Wizard Zorander. It is of vital importance that I have your help. As I've already told you, the lives of innocent children are at stake.'

Wizard Zorander finally peered up. After appraising her a long moment he straightened. 'Where does the line lie?'

Abby glanced to the sorceress on one side of her and then the Mother Confessor on the other side. Neither looked back.

'Excuse me, Wizard Zorander? The line?'

The wizard's brow drew down. 'You imply a higher value to a life because of a young age. The line, my dear child, across which the value of life becomes petty. Where is the line?'

'But a child—'

He held up a cautionary finger. 'Do not think to play on my emotions by plying me with the value of the life of a child, as if a higher value can be placed on life because of age. When is life worth less? Where is the line? At what age? Who decides?

'All life is of value. Dead is dead, no matter the age. Don't think to produce a suspension of my reason with a callous, calculated twisting of emotion, like some slippery officeholder stirring the passions of a mindless mob.'

Abby was struck speechless by such an admonition. The wizard turned his attention to the Mother Confessor.

'Speaking of bureaucrats, what did the council have to say for themselves?'

The Mother Confessor clasped her hands and sighed. 'I told them your words. Simply put, they didn't care. They want it done.'

He grunted his discontent. 'Do they, now?' His hazel eyes turned to Abby. 'Seems the council doesn't care about the lives of even children, when the children are D'Haran.' He wiped a hand across his tired-looking eyes. 'I can't say I don't comprehend their reasoning, or that I disagree with them, but dear spirits, they are not the ones to do it. It is not by their hand. It will be by mine.'

'I understand, Zedd,' the Mother Confessor murmured.

Once again he seemed to notice Abby standing before him. He considered her as if pondering some profound notion. It made her fidget. He held out his hand and waggled his fingers. 'Let me see it, then.'

Abby stepped closer to the table as she reached in her sack.

'If you cannot be persuaded to help innocent people, then maybe this will mean something more to you.'

She drew her mother's skull from the sack and placed it in the wizard's upturned palm. 'It is a debt of bones. I declare it due.'

One eyebrow lifted. 'It is customary to bring only a tiny fragment of bone, child.'

Abby felt her face flush. 'I didn't know,' she stammered. 'I wanted to be sure there was enough to test ... to be sure you would believe me.'

He smoothed a gentle hand over the top of the skull. 'A piece smaller than a grain of sand is enough.' He watched Abby's eyes. 'Didn't your mother tell you?'

Abby shook her head. 'She said only that it was a debt passed to you from your father. She said the debt must be paid if it was called due.'

'Indeed it must,' he whispered.

Zedd pulled his heavy chair forward and sat at his desk to examine Abby's terrible treasure. She watched with bated breath as his hand glided back and forth over her mother's skull. The bone was dull and stained by the dirt from which Abby had pulled it, not at all the pristine white she had fancied it would be. It had horrified her to have to uncover her mother's bones, but the alternative horrified her more.

Beneath the wizard's fingers, the bone of the skull began to glow with soft amber light. Abby's breathing nearly stilled when the air hummed, as if the spirits themselves whispered to the wizard. The sorceress fussed with the beads at her neck. The Mother Confessor chewed her lower lip. Abby prayed.

Wizard Zorander set the skull on his desk and stood, turning his back on them. The amber glow faded away.

When he said nothing, Abby spoke into the thick silence. 'Well? Are you satisfied? Did your test prove it a debt true?'

'Oh yes,' he said quietly without turning towards them. 'It is a debt of bones true, bound by the magic invoked until the debt is paid.'

Abby's fingers worried at the frayed edge of her sack. 'I told you. My mother wouldn't have lied to me. She told me that if not paid while she was alive, it became a debt of bones upon her death.'

The wizard slowly rounded to face her. 'And did she tell you anything of the engendering of the debt?'

'No.' Abby cast a furtive, sidelong glance at Delora before going on. 'Sorceresses hold secrets close, and reveal only that which serves their purposes.'

With a slight, fleeting smile, he grunted his concurrence.

'She said only that it was your father and she who were

bound in it, and that until paid it would continue to pass on to the descendants of each.'

'Your mother spoke the truth. But that does not mean that it must be paid now.'

'It is a solemn debt of bones.' Abby's frustration and fear erupted with venom. 'I declare it due! You will yield to the obligation!'

Both the sorceress and the Mother Confessor gazed off at the walls, uneasy at a woman, an ungifted woman, raising her voice to the First Wizard himself. Abby suddenly wondered if she might be struck dead for such insolence. But if he didn't help her, it wouldn't matter.

The Mother Confessor diverted the possible results of Abby's outburst with a question. 'Zedd, did your reading tell you of the nature of the engendering of the debt?'

'Indeed it did,' he said. 'My father, too, told me of a debt. My test has proven to me that this is the one of which he spoke, and that the woman standing before me carries the other half of the link.'

'So, what was the engendering?' the sorceress asked.

'It seems to have slipped my mind.' He turned his palms up as he flashed the sorceress a brief, innocent expression. 'I'm sorry; I find myself to be more forgetful than usual of late.'

Delora sniffed. 'And you dare to call sorceresses taciturn?'

Wizard Zorander absently considered her a moment before turning a resolute visage on the Mother Confessor. 'The council wants it done, do they?' He smiled a grim, sly smile. 'Then it shall be done.'

The Mother Confessor cocked her head. 'Zedd . . . are you sure about this?'

'About what?' Abby asked. 'Are you going to honour the debt or not?'

The wizard shrugged. 'You have declared the debt due.' He plucked a small book from the table and slipped it into a pocket in his robe. 'Who am I to argue?'

'Dear spirits,' the Mother Confessor whispered to herself. 'Zedd, just because the council—'

'I am just a wizard,' he said, cutting her off, 'serving the wants and wishes of the people.'

'But if you travel to this place you would be exposing yourself to needless danger.'

'I must be near the border – or it will claim parts of the Midlands, too. Coney Crossing is as good a place as any other to ignite the conflagration.'

Beside herself with relief, Abby was hardly hearing anything else he said. 'Thank you, Wizard Zorander. Thank you.'

He strode around the table and gripped her shoulder with stick-like fingers of surprising strength.

'We are bound, you and I, in a debt of bones. Our life paths have intersected.' His smile looked at once sad and sincere. His powerful fingers closed around her wrist, around her bracelet, and he put her mother's skull in her hands. 'Please, Abby, call me Zedd.'

Near tears, she nodded. 'Thank you, Zedd.'

Outside, in the early light, they were accosted by the waiting crowd. Wizard Thomas, waving his papers, shoved his way through.

'Zorander! I've been studying these elements you've provided. I have to talk to you.'

'Talk, then,' the First Wizard said as he marched by. The crowd followed in his wake.

'This is madness.'

'I never said it wasn't.'

Wizard Thomas shook the papers as if for proof. 'You can't do this, Zorander!'

'The council has decided that it is to be done. The war must be ended while we have the upper hand and before Panis Rahl comes up with something we won't be able to counter.'

'No, I mean I've studied this thing, and you won't be able to do it. We don't understand the power those wizards wielded. I've looked over the elements you've shown me. Even trying to invoke such a thing will create intense heat.'

Zedd halted and put his face close to Thomas. He lifted his eyebrows in mock surprise. 'Really, Thomas? Do you think? Igniting a light spell that will rip the fabric of the world of life might cause an instability in the elements of the web field?'

Thomas charged after as Zedd stormed off. 'Zorander! You won't be able to control it! If you were able to invoke it – and I'm not saying I believe you can – you would breach the Grace. The invocation uses heat. The breach feeds it. You won't be able to control the cascade. No one can do such a thing!'

'I can do it,' the First Wizard muttered.

Thomas shook the fists of papers in a fury. 'Zorander, your arrogance will be the end of us all! Once parted, the veil will be rent and all life will be consumed. I demand to see the book in which you found this spell. I demand to see it myself. The whole thing, not just parts of it!'

The First Wizard paused and lifted a finger. 'Thomas, if you were meant to see the book, then you would be

First Wizard and have access to the First Wizard's private enclave. But you are not, and you don't.'

Thomas's face glowed scarlet above his white beard. 'This is a foolhardy act of desperation!'

Wizard Zorander flicked the finger. The papers flew from the old wizard's hand and swirled up into a whirlwind, there to ignite, flaring into ashes that lifted away on the wind.

'Sometimes, Thomas, all that is left to you is an act of desperation. I am First Wizard, and I will do as I must. That is the end of it. I will hear no more.' He turned and snatched the sleeve of an officer. 'Alert the lancers. Gather all the cavalry available. We ride for Pendisan Reach at once.'

The man thumped a quick salute to his chest before dashing off. Another officer, older and looking to be of much higher rank, cleared his throat.

'Wizard Zorander, may I know of your plan?'

'It is Anargo,' the First Wizard said, 'who is the right hand of Panis Rahl, and in conjunction with Rahl conjures death to stalk us. Quite simply put, I intend to send death back at them.'

'By leading the lancers into Pendisan Reach?'

'Yes. Anargo holds at Coney Crossing. We have General Brainard driving north towards Pendisan Reach, General Sanderson sweeping south to join with him, and Mardale charging up from the southwest. We will go in there with the lancers and whoever of the rest of them is able to join with us.'

'Anargo is no fool. We don't know how many other wizards and gifted he has with him, but we know what they're capable of. They've bled us time and time again.

66

At last we have dealt them a blow.' The officer chose his words carefully. 'Why do you think they wait? Why wouldn't they simply slip back into D'Hara?'

Zedd rested a hand on the crenellated wall and gazed out on the dawn, out on the city below.

'Anargo relishes the game. He performs it with high drama; he wants us to think them wounded. Pendisan Reach is the only terrain in all those mountains that an army can get through with any speed. Coney Crossing provides a wide field for battle, but not wide enough to let us manoeuvre easily, or flank them. He is trying to bait us in.'

The officer didn't seem surprised. 'But why?'

Zedd looked back over his shoulder at the man. 'Obviously, he believes that in such terrain he can defeat us. I believe otherwise. He knows that we can't allow the menace to remain there, and he knows our plans. He thinks to draw me in, kill me, and end the threat I alone hold over them.'

'So . . .' the officer reasoned aloud, 'you are saying that for Anargo, it is worth the risk.'

Zedd stared out once more at the city below the Wizard's Keep. 'If Anargo is right, he could win it all at Coney Crossing. When he has finished me, he will turn his gifted loose, slaughter the bulk of our forces all in one place, and then, virtually unopposed, cut out the heart of the Midlands: Aydindril.

'Anargo plans that before the snow flies, he will have killed me, annihilated our joint forces, have the people of the Midlands in chains, and be able to hand the whip to Panis Rahl.'

The officer stared, dumbfounded. 'And you plan to do as Anargo is hoping and go in there to face him?'

Zedd shrugged. 'What choice have I?'

'And do you at least know how Anargo plans to kill you, so that we might take precautions? Take countermeasures?'

'I'm afraid not.' Vexed, he waved his hand, dismissing the matter. He turned to Abby. 'The lancers have swift horses. We will ride hard. We will be to your home soon – we will be there in time – and then we'll see to our business.'

Abby only nodded. She couldn't put into words the relief of her petition granted, nor could she express the shame she felt to have her prayer answered. But most of all, she couldn't utter a word of her horror at what she was doing, for she knew the D'Harans' plan.

Flies swarmed around dried scraps of viscera, all that was left of Abby's prized bearded pigs. Apparently, even the breeding stock, which Abby's parents had given her as a wedding gift, had been slaughtered and taken.

Abby's parents, too, had chosen Abby's husband. Abby had never met him before: he came from the town of Lynford where her mother and father bought the pigs. Abby had been beside herself with anxiety over who her parents would choose for her husband. She had hoped for a man who would be of good cheer – a man to bring a smile to the difficulties of life.

When she first saw Philip, she thought he must be the most serious man in all the world. His young face looked to her as if it had never once smiled. That first night after meeting him, she had cried herself to sleep over thoughts of sharing her life with so solemn a man. She thought her life caught up on the sharp tines of grim fate.

Abby came to find that Philip was a hardworking man who looked out at life through a great grin. That first day she had seen him, she only later learned, he had been putting on his most sober face so that his new family would not think him a slacker unworthy of their daughter. In a short time, Abby had come to know that Philip was a man upon whom she could depend. By the time Jana had been born, she had come to love him.

Now Philip, and so many others, depended upon her.

Abby brushed her hands clean after putting her mother's bones to rest once more. The fences Jana had watched Philip so often mend, she saw, were all broken down. Coming back around the house, she noticed that barn doors were missing. Anything an animal or human could eat was gone. Abby could not recall having ever seen her home looking so barren.

It didn't matter, she told herself. It didn't matter, if only Jana would be returned to her. Fences could be mended. Pigs could be replaced, somehow, someday. Jana could never be replaced.

'Abby,' Zedd asked as he peered around at the ruins of her home, 'how is it that you weren't taken, when your husband and daughter and everyone else were?'

Abby stepped through the broken doorway, thinking that her home had never looked so small. Before she had gone to Aydindril, to the Wizard's Keep, her home had seemed as big as anything she could imagine. Here, Philip had laughed and filled the simple room with his comfort and conversation. With charcoal he had drawn animals on the stone hearth for Jana.

Abby pointed. 'Under that door is the root cellar. That's where I was when I heard the things I told you about.'

Zedd ran the toe of his boot across the knothole used as a finger-hold to lift the hatch. 'They were taking your husband, and your daughter, and you stayed down there? While your daughter was screaming for you, you didn't run up to help her?'

Abby summoned her voice. 'I knew that if I came up, they would have me, too. I knew that the only chance my family had was if I waited and then went for help. My mother always told me that even a sorceress was no more than a fool if she acted like one. She always told me to think things through, first.'

'Wise advice.' Zedd set down a ladle that had been bent and holed. He rested a gentle hand on her shoulder. 'It would have been hard to leave your daughter crying for you, and do the wise thing instead.'

Abby could only manage a whisper. 'You speak the spirits' own truth.' She pointed out the window. 'That way – across the Coney River – lies town. They took Jana and Philip with them as they went on to take all the people from town. They had others, too, that they had already captured. The army set up camp in the hills beyond the river.'

Zedd stood for a time, silently gazing out at the distant hills. When he finally spoke, it seemed he was speaking more to himself than to her. 'Soon, I hope, this war will be ended. Dear spirits, let it end.'

Remembering the Mother Confessor's admonition not to repeat the story she told, Abby never asked about the wizard's daughter or murdered wife. When on their swift journey back to Coney Crossing she spoke of her love for Jana, it must have broken his heart to think of his own daughter in the brutal hands of the same enemy, knowing that he had left her to face death lest many more die.

Zedd pushed open the bedroom door. 'And back here?' he asked as he put his head into the room beyond.

Abby looked up from her thoughts. 'The bedroom. In the rear is a door back to the garden and the barn.'

Though he never once mentioned his dead wife or missing daughter, Abby's knowledge of them ate away at her like a swelling spring river ate at a hole in the ice.

Zedd stepped back in from the bedroom as Delora came silently slipping in through the front doorway. 'As Abigail said, the town across the river has been sacked,' the sorceress reported. 'From the looks of it, the people were all taken.'

Zedd brushed back his wavy hair. 'How close is the river?'

Abby gestured out the window. Night was falling. 'Just there. A walk of only a few minutes.'

In the valley, on its way to join the Kern, the Coney River slowed and spread wide, so that it became shallow enough to cross easily. There was no bridge; the road simply led to the river's edge and took up again on the other side. Though the river was near to a quarter-mile across in most of the valley, it was in no place much more than knee-deep. Only in the spring melt was it occasionally treacherous to cross. The town of Coney Crossing was two miles beyond, up on the rise of hills, safe from spring floods, as was the knoll where Abby's farmyard stood.

Zedd took Delora by the elbow. 'Ride back and tell

everyone to hold station. If anything goes wrong . . . well, if anything goes wrong, then they must attack. Anargo's legion must be stopped, even if they have to go into D'Hara after them.'

Delora did not look pleased. 'Before we left, the Mother Confessor made me promise that I would be sure that you were not left alone. She told me to see to it that gifted were always near if you needed them.'

Abby, too, had heard the Mother Confessor issue the orders. Looking back at the Keep as they had crossed the stone bridge, Abby had seen the Mother Confessor upon a high rampart, watching them leave. The Mother Confessor had helped when Abby had feared all was lost. She wondered what would become of the woman.

Then she remembered she didn't have to wonder. She knew.

The wizard ignored what the sorceress had said. 'As soon as I help Abby, I'll send her back, too. I don't want anyone near when I unleash the spell.'

Delora gripped his collar and pulled him close. She looked as if she might be about to give him a heated scolding. Instead she drew him into an embrace.

'Please, Zedd,' she whispered, 'don't leave us without you as First Wizard.'

Zedd smoothed back her dark hair. 'And abandon you all to Thomas?' He smirked. 'Never.'

The dust from Delora's horse drifted away into the gathering darkness as Zedd and Abby descended the slope towards the river. Abby led him along the path through the tall grasses and rushes, explaining that the path would offer them better concealment than the road. Abby was thankful that he didn't argue for the road.

Her eyes darted from the deep shadows on one side to the shadows on the other as they were swallowed into the brush. Her pulse raced. She flinched whenever a twig snapped underfoot.

It happened as she feared it would, as she knew it would.

A figure enfolded in a long hooded cloak darted out of nowhere, knocking Abby aside. She saw the flash of a blade as Zedd flipped the attacker into the brush. He squatted, putting a hand back on Abby's shoulder as she lay in the grass panting.

'Stay down,' he whispered urgently.

Light gathered at his fingers. He was conjuring magic. That was what they wanted him to do.

Tears welled, burning her eyes. She snatched his sleeve. 'Zedd, don't use magic.' She could hardly speak past the tightening pain in her chest. 'Don't—'

The figure sprang again from the gloom of the bushes. Zedd threw up a hand. The night lit with a flash of hot light that struck the cloaked figure.

Rather than the assailant going down, it was Zedd who cried out and crumpled to the ground. Whatever he had thought to do to the attacker, it had been turned back on him, and he was in the grip of the most terrible anguish, preventing him from rising, or speaking. That was why they had wanted him to conjure magic: so they could capture him.

The figure standing over the wizard glowered at Abby. 'Your part here is finished. Go.'

Abby scuttled into the grass. The woman pushed the hood back, and cast off her cloak. In the near darkness, Abby could see the woman's long braid and red leather uniform. It was one of the women Abby had been told about, the women used to capture those with magic: the Mord-Sith.

The Mord-Sith watched with satisfaction as the wizard at her feet writhed in choking pain. 'Well, well. Looks like the First Wizard himself has just made a very big mistake.'

The belts and straps of her red leather uniform creaked as she leaned down towards him, grinning at his agony. 'I have been given the whole night to make you regret ever having lifted a finger to resist us. In the morning I'm to allow you to watch as our forces annihilate your people. Afterwards, I am to take you to Lord Rahl himself, the man who ordered the death of your wife, so you can beg him to order me to kill you, too.' She kicked him. 'So you can beg Lord Rahl for your death, as you watch your daughter die before your eyes.'

Zedd could only scream in horror and pain.

On her hands and knees, Abby crabbed her way farther back into the weeds and rushes. She wiped at her eyes, trying to see. She was horrified to witness what was being done to the man who had agreed to help her for no more reason than a debt to her mother. By contrast, these people had coerced her service by holding hostage the life of her child.

As she backed away, Abby saw the knife the Mord-Sith had dropped when Zedd had thrown her into the weeds. The knife was a pretext, used to provoke him to act; it was magic that was the true weapon. The Mord-Sith had used his own magic against him – used it to cripple and capture him, and now used it to hurt him.

74

It was the price demanded. Abby had complied. She had no choice.

But what toll was she imposing on others?

How could she save her daughter's life at the cost of so many others? Would Jana grow up to be a slave to people who would do this? With a mother who would allow it? Jana would grow up to learn to bow to Panis Rahl and his minions, to submit to evil, or worse, grow up to become a willing party to the scourge, never tasting liberty or knowing the value of honour.

With dreadful finality, everything seemed to fall to ruin in Abby's mind.

She snatched up the knife. Zedd was wailing in pain as the Mord-Sith bent, doing some foul thing to him. Before she had time to lose her resolve, Abby was moving towards the woman's back.

Abby had butchered animals. She told herself that this was no different. These were not people, but animals. She lifted the knife.

A hand clamped over her mouth. Another seized her wrist.

Abby moaned against the hand, against her failure to stop this madness when she had had the chance. A mouth close to her ear urged her to hush.

Struggling against the figure in a hooded cloak that held her, Abby turned her head as much as she could, and in the last of the daylight saw violet eyes looking back. For a moment she couldn't make sense of it, couldn't make sense of how the woman could be there when Abby had seen her remain behind. But it truly was her.

Abby stilled. The Mother Confessor released her and with a quick hand signal, urged her back. Abby didn't question; she scurried back into the rushes as the Mother Confessor slipped through the spectral shadows, closer to the woman in red leather. The Mord-Sith was bent over, intent on her grisly business with the screaming wizard.

In the distance, bugs chirped and clicked. The Mother Confessor reached toward the figure in red. Frogs called with insistent croaks, oblivious to Zedd's heart-wrenching agony. Not far away the river sloshed and burbled as it always did – a familiar, comforting sound of home that this night brought no comfort.

The gentle fingers that had once gentled Abby's brow finally found the woman in red leather. For an instant, Abby feared the wicked woman might pull away from the touch and reel around to unleash her violence on the Mother Confessor.

And then there came a sudden, violent concussion to the air. Thunder without sound. It drove the wind from Abby's lungs. The wallop nearly knocked her senseless, making every joint in her body burn in sharp pain.

There was no flash of light – just that pure and flawless jolt to the air. The world seemed to stop in its terrible splendour.

Grass flattened as if in a wind radiating out in a ring from the Mord-Sith and the Mother Confessor. Abby's senses returned as the pain in her joints thankfully melted away.

Abby had never seen it done before, and had never expected to see it in the whole of her life, but she knew without doubt that she had just witnessed a Confessor unleashing her power. From what Abby's mother had told her, it was the destruction of a person's mind so complete that it left only numb devotion to the Confessor. She had but to ask and they would confess any truth, no matter the crime they had previously attempted to conceal or deny.

'Mistress,' the Mord-Sith moaned in piteous lamentation.

Abby, first staggered by the shock of the soundless thunder of the Mother Confessor's power, and now stunned by the abject anguish of the woman crumpled on the ground, started when a hand gripped her arm. She sagged with relief when she saw it was the wizard.

With the back of his other hand he wiped blood from his mouth. He laboured to get his breath. 'Leave her to it.'

'Zedd . . . I . . . I'm so sorry. I tried to tell you not to use magic, but I didn't call loud enough for you to hear.'

He managed to smile through obvious pain. 'I heard you.'

'But why then did you use your gift?'

'I thought that in the end, you would not be the kind of person to do such a terrible thing, and that you would show your true heart.' He pulled her away from the cries. 'We used you. We wanted them to think they had succeeded.'

'You knew what I was going to do? You knew I was to bring you to them so that they could capture you?'

'I had a good idea. From the first there seemed more to you than you presented. You are not very talented at being a spy and a traitor. Since we arrived here you've been watching the shadows and jumping at the chirp of every bug.'

The Mother Confessor rushed up. 'Zedd, are you all right?'

He put a hand on her shoulder. 'I'll be fine.' His eyes

still held the glaze of terror. 'Thank you for not being late. For a moment, I feared . . .'

'I know.' The Mother Confessor offered a quick smile. 'Let us hope your trick was worth it. You have until dawn. She said they expect her to torture you all night before bringing you to them in the morning. Their scouts alerted Anargo to our troops' arrival.'

Back in the rushes the Mord-Sith was screaming as though she were being flayed alive.

Shivers ran through Abby's shoulders. 'They'll hear her and know what's happened.'

'Even if they could hear at this distance, they will think it is Zedd, being tortured by her.' The Mother Confessor took the knife from Abby's hand. 'I am glad that you rewarded my faith and in the end chose not to join with them.'

Abby wiped her palms on her skirts, shamed by all she had done, by what she had intended to do. She was beginning to shake. 'Are you going to kill her?'

The Mother Confessor, despite looking bone-weary after having touched the Mord-Sith, still had iron resolve in her eyes. 'A Mord-Sith is different from anyone else. She does not recover from the touch of a Confessor. She would suffer in profound agony until she dies, sometime before morning.' She glanced back towards the cries. 'She has told us what we need to know, and Zedd must have his power back. It is the merciful thing to do.'

'It also buys me time to do what I must do.' Zedd's fingers turned Abby's face towards him, away from the shrieks. 'And time to get Jana back. You will have until morning.'

'I will have until morning? What do you mean?'

'I'll explain. But we must hurry if you are to have enough time. Now, take off your clothes.'

Abby was running out of time.

She moved through the D'Haran camp, holding herself stiff and tall, trying not to look frantic, even though that was how she felt. All night long she had been doing as the wizard had instructed: acting haughty. To anyone who noticed her, she directed disdain. To anyone who looked her way, thinking to speak to her, she growled.

Not that many, though, so much as dared to catch the attention of what appeared to be a red-leather-clad Mord-Sith. Zedd had told her, too, to keep the Mord-Sith's weapon in her fist. It looked like nothing more than a small red leather rod. How it worked, Abby had no idea – the wizard had said only that it involved magic, and she wouldn't be able to call it to her aid – but it did have an effect on those who saw it in her hand: it made them melt back into the darkness, away from the light of the campfires, away from Abby.

Those who were awake, anyway. Although most people in the camp were sleeping, there was no shortage of alert guards. Zedd had cut the long braid from the Mord-Sith who had attacked him, and tied it into Abby's hair. In the dark, the mismatch of colour wasn't obvious. When the guards looked at Abby they saw a Mord-Sith, and quickly turned their attention elsewhere.

By the apprehension on people's faces when they saw her coming, Abby knew she must look fearsome. They didn't know how her heart pounded. She was thankful for the mantle of night so that the D'Harans couldn't see her knees trembling. She had seen only two real Mord-Sith, both sleeping, and she had kept far away from them, as Zedd had warned her. Real Mord-Sith were not likely to be fooled so easily.

Zedd had given her until dawn. Time was running out. He had told her that if she wasn't back in time, she would die.

Abby was thankful she knew the lay of the land, or long since she would have become lost among the confusion of tents, campfires, wagons, horses, and mules. Everywhere pikes and lances were stacked upright in circles with their points leaning together. Men – farriers, fletchers, blacksmiths and craftsmen of all sorts – worked through the night.

The air was thick with woodsmoke and rang with the sound of metal being shaped and sharpened and wood being worked for everything from bows to wagons. Abby didn't know how people could sleep through the noise, but sleep they did.

Shortly the immense camp would wake to a new day – a day of battle, a day the soldiers went to work doing what they did best. They were getting a good night's sleep so they would be rested for the killing of the Midlands army. From what she had heard, D'Haran soldiers were very good at their job.

Abby had searched relentlessly, but she had been unable to find her father, her husband, or her daughter. She had no intention of giving up. She had resigned herself to the knowledge that if she didn't find them, she would die with them.

She had found captives tied together and staked to trees, or the ground, to keep them from running. Many

more were chained. Some she recognized, but many more she didn't. Most were kept in groups and under guard.

Abby never once saw a guard asleep at his post. When they looked her way, she acted as if she were looking for someone, and she wasn't going to go easy on them when she found them. Zedd had told her that her safety, and the safety of her family, depended on her playing the part convincingly. Abby thought about these people hurting her daughter, and it wasn't hard to act angry.

But she was running out of time. She couldn't find them, and she knew that Zedd would not wait. Too much was at stake; she understood that, now. She was coming to appreciate that the wizard and the Mother Confessor were trying to stop a war; that they were people resolved to the dreadful task of weighing the lives of a few against the lives of many.

Abby lifted another tent-flap, and saw soldiers sleeping. She squatted and looked at the faces of prisoners tied to wagons. They stared back with hollow expressions. She bent to gaze at the faces of children pressed together in nightmares. She couldn't find Jana. The huge camp sprawled across the hilly countryside; there were a thousand places she could be.

As she marched along a crooked line of tents, she scratched at her wrist. Only when she went farther did she notice that it was the bracelet warming that made her wrist itch. It warmed yet more as she proceeded, but then the warmth began fading. Her brow twitched and her heart beat faster as she considered what it could possibly mean. Fearing to hope that it could be the help she so desperately needed, yet unwilling to abandon that hope, she turned and went back toward where the bracelet had inexplicably given off heat.

Where a pathway between tents turned off, her bracelet tingled again with warmth. Abby paused a moment, looking off into the darkness. The sky was just beginning to colour with light. She took the path between the tents, following until the bracelet cooled, then backtracked to where it warmed again and took a new direction where it warmed yet more.

Abby's mother had given her the bracelet, telling her to wear it always, and that someday it would be of value. Abby wondered if somehow the bracelet had magic that would help her find her daughter. With dawn nearing, this seemed the only chance she had left. She hurried onward, wending where the warmth from the bracelet directed.

The bracelet led her to an expanse of snoring soldiers. There were no prisoners in sight. Guards patrolled the men in bedrolls and blankets. There was one tent set among the big men – for an officer, she guessed.

Not knowing what else to do, Abby strode among the sleeping men. Near the tent, the bracelet sent tingling heat up her arm.

Abby saw that sentries hung around the small tent like flies around meat. The canvas sides glowed softly, probably from a candle inside. Off to the side, she noticed a sleeping form different from the men. As she got closer, she saw that it was a woman: Mariska.

The old woman breathed with a little raspy whistle as she slept. Abby stood paralysed. Guards looked up at her.

Needing to do something before they asked any questions, Abby scowled at them and marched towards the tent. She tried not to make any noise; the guards might think she was a Mord-Sith, but Mariska would not long be fooled. A glare from Abby turned the guards' eyes to the dark countryside.

Her heart pounding nearly out of control, Abby gripped the tent-flap. She knew Jana would be inside. She told herself that she must not cry out when she saw her daughter. She reminded herself that she must put a hand over Jana's mouth before she could cry out with joy, lest they be caught before they had a chance to escape.

The bracelet was so hot it felt as if it would blister her skin. Abby ducked into the low tent.

The light of a single candle revealed a trembling little girl huddled in a tattered wool cloak, sitting amid rumpled blankets. She took in the red leather and then stared up with big eyes that blinked with terror of what might come next. Abby felt a stab of anguish. It was not Jana.

They shared a rapt look, this little girl and Abby, of emotions beyond words. The child's face, as Abby's must have been, was lit clearly by the candle set to the side. In those big grey eyes that looked to have beheld unimaginable terrors, the little girl seemed to reach a judgement.

Her arms stretched up in supplication.

Instinctively, protectively, Abby fell to her knees and scooped up the child, hugging her small trembling body. The girl's spindly arms came out from the tattered cloak and wrapped around Abby's neck, holding on for dear life.

'Help me? Please?' the child whimpered in Abby's ear.

Before she had picked her up she had seen the face in the candlelight. There was no doubt in Abby's mind. It was Zedd's daughter.

'I've come to help you,' Abby comforted. 'Zedd sent me.'

The child moaned expectantly at hearing the beloved name.

Abby held the girl out at arm's length. 'I'll take you to your father, but you mustn't let these people know I'm rescuing you. Can you play along with me? Can you pretend that you're my prisoner, so that I can get you away?'

Near tears, the girl nodded. She had the same wavy hair as Zedd, and the same eyes, although they were an arresting grey, not hazel.

'Good,' Abby whispered, cupping a chilly cheek, almost lost in those grey eyes. 'Trust me, then, and I will get you away.'

'I trust you,' came the small voice.

Abby snatched up a rope lying nearby and looped it around the girl's neck. 'I'll try not to hurt you, but I must make them think you are my prisoner.'

The girl cast a worried look at the rope, as if she knew it well, and then nodded that she would go along.

Abby stood, once outside the tent, and by the rope pulled the child out after her. The guards looked her way. Abby started out.

One of them scowled as he stepped close. 'What's going on?'

Abby stomped to a halt and lifted the red leather rod, pointing it at the guard's nose. 'She has been summoned. And who are you to question? Get out of my way or I'll have you gutted and cleaned for my breakfast!'

The man paled and hurriedly stepped aside. Before he had time to reconsider, Abby charged off, the girl in tow at the end of the rope, dragging her heels, making it look real.

No one followed. Abby wanted to run, but she couldn't. She wanted to carry the girl, but she couldn't. It had to look as if a Mord-Sith was taking a prisoner away.

Rather than take the shortest route back to Zedd, Abby followed the hills upriver to a place where the trees offered concealment almost to the water's edge. Zedd had told her where to cross, and warned her not to return by a different way; he had set traps of magic to prevent the D'Harans from charging down from the hills to stop whatever it was he was going to do.

Closer to the river she saw, downstream a way, a bank of fog hanging close to the ground. Zedd had emphatically warned her not to go near any fog. She suspected it a poison cloud of some sort that he had conjured.

The sound of the water told her she was close to the river. The pink sky provided enough light to finally see it when she reached the edge of the trees. Although she could see the massive camp on the hills in the distance behind her, she saw no one following.

Abby took the rope from the child's neck. The girl watched her with those big round eyes. Abby lifted her and held her tight.

'Hold on, and keep quiet.'

Pressing the girl's head to her shoulder, Abby ran for the river.

There was light, but it was not the dawn. They had crossed the frigid water and made the other side when she first noticed it. Even as she ran along the bank of the river, before she could see the source of the light, Abby knew that magic was being called there that was unlike any magic she had ever seen before. A sound, low and thin, whined up the river towards her. A smell, as if the air itself had been burned, hung along the riverbank.

The little girl clung to Abby, tears running down her face, afraid to speak – afraid, it seemed, to hope that she had at last been rescued, as if asking a question might somehow make it all vanish like a dream upon waking. Abby felt tears coursing down her own cheeks.

When she rounded a bend in the river, she spotted the wizard. He stood in the centre of the river, on a rock that Abby had never before seen. The rock was just large enough to clear the surface of the water by a few inches, making it almost appear as if the wizard stood on the surface of the water.

Before him as he faced towards distant D'Hara, shapes, dark and wavering, floated in the air. They curled around, as if confiding in him, conversing, warning, tempting him with floating arms and reaching fingers that wreathed like smoke.

Animate light twisted up around the wizard. Colours both dark and wondrous glimmered about him, cavorting with the shadowy forms undulating through the air. It was at once the most enchanting and the most frightening thing Abby had ever seen. No magic her mother conjured had ever seemed ... aware.

But the most frightening thing by far was what hovered in the air before the wizard. It appeared to be a molten sphere, so hot it glowed from within, its surface a crackling of fluid dross. An arm of water from the river magically turned skyward in a fountain spray, and poured down over the rotating silvery mass.

The water hissed and steamed as it hit the sphere, leaving behind clouds of white vapour to drift away in the gentle dawn wind. The molten form blackened at the touch of the water cascading over it, and yet the intense inner heat melted the glassy surface again as fast as the water cooled it, making the whole thing bubble and boil in mid-air, a pulsing sinister menace.

Transfixed, Abby let the child slip to the silty ground. The little girl's arms stretched out. 'Papa.'

He was too far away to hear her, but he heard.

Zedd turned, at once larger than life in the midst of magic Abby could see but not begin to fathom, yet at the same time small with the frailty of human need. Tears filled his eyes as he gazed at his daughter standing beside Abby. This man who seemed to be consulting with spirits looked as if for the first time he were seeing a true apparition.

Zedd leaped off the rock and charged through the water. When he reached her and swept her up into the safety of his arms, she began to wail at last with the contained terror released.

'There, there, dear one,' Zedd comforted. 'Papa is here now.'

'Oh, Papa,' she cried against his neck, 'they hurt Mama. They were wicked. They hurt her so . . .'

He hushed her tenderly. 'I know, dear one. I know.'

For the first time, Abby saw the sorceress and the Mother Confessor standing off to the side, watching, their eyes glistening with tears. Though Abby was glad for the wizard and his daughter, the sight only intensified the hot pain in her chest at what she had lost. The choking anguish fed her tears.

'There, there, dear one,' Zedd was cooing. 'You're safe, now. Papa won't let anything happen to you. You're safe now.'

Zedd turned to Abby. By the time he had smiled his tearful appreciation, the child was asleep.

'A little spell,' he explained when Abby's brow twitched with surprise. 'She needs to rest. I need to finish what I am doing.'

He put his daughter in Abby's arms. 'Abby, would you take her up to your house where she can sleep until I'm finished here? Please, put her in bed and cover her up to keep her warm. She will sleep for now.'

Thinking about her own daughter in the hands of the brutes across the river, Abby could only nod before turning to the task. She was happy for Zedd, and even felt pride at having rescued his little girl, but as she ran for her home, she was near to dying with grief over her failure to recover her own family.

Abby settled the dead weight of the sleeping child into her bed. She drew the curtain across the small window in her bedroom, and unable to resist, smoothed back silky hair and pressed a kiss to the soft brow before leaving the girl to her blessed rest.

With the child safe at last and asleep, Abby raced back down the knoll to the river. She thought to ask Zedd to give her just a little more time so she could return to look for her own daughter. Fear for Jana had her heart pounding wildly. He owed her a debt, and had not yet seen it through.

Wringing her hands, Abby came to a panting halt at the water's edge. She watched the wizard up on his rock in the river, light and shadow coursing up around him. She had been around magic enough to have the sense to fear approaching him. She could hear his chanted words; though they were words she had never before heard, she recognized the idiosyncratic cadence of words spoken in a spell, words calling together frightful forces.

On the ground beside her was the strange Grace she had seen him draw before, the one that breached the worlds of life and death. The Grace was drawn with a sparkling, pure white sand that stood out in stark relief against the dark silt. Abby shuddered even to look upon it, much less contemplate its meaning. Around the Grace, carefully drawn with the same sparkling white sand, were geometric forms of magical invocations.

Abby lowered her fists, about to call out to the wizard, when Delora leaned close. Abby flinched in surprise.

'Not now, Abigail,' the sorceress murmured. 'Don't disturb him in the middle of this part.'

Reluctantly, Abby heeded the sorceress's words. The Mother Confessor was there, too. Abby chewed her bottom lip as she watched the wizard throw up his arms. Sparkles of coloured light curled up along twisting shafts of shadows. 'But I must. I haven't been able to find my family. He must help me. He must save them. It's a debt of bones that must be satisfied.'

The other two women shared a look. 'Abby,' the Mother Confessor said, 'he gave you a chance, gave you time. He tried. He did his best, but he has everyone else to think of, now.'

The Mother Confessor took up Abby's hand, and the sorceress put an arm around Abby's shoulders as she stood weeping on the riverbank. Despair crushed her. It wasn't supposed to end this way, not after all she had been through, not after all she had done.

The wizard, his arms raised, called forth more light, more shadows, more magic. The river roiled around him. The hissing thing in the air grew as it slowly slumped closer to the water. Shafts of light shot from the hot, rotating, bloom of power.

The sun was rising over the hills behind the D'Harans. This part of the river wasn't as wide as elsewhere, and Abby could see the activity in the trees beyond. Men moved about, but the fog hanging on the far bank kept them wary, kept them in the trees.

Also across the river, at the edge of the tree-covered hills, another wizard appeared. He threw down a rock and then leaped atop it. He pushed up the sleeves of his robes and flung his arms skyward, launching sparkling light up into the air. Abby thought that the strong morning sun might outshine the conjured illuminations, but it didn't.

Abby could stand it no longer. 'Zedd!' she called out across the river. 'Zedd! Please, you promised! I found your daughter! What about mine? Please don't do this until she is safe!'

Zedd turned and looked at her as if from a great distance, as if from another world. Arms of dark forms caressed him. Fingers of dark smoke dragged along his jaw, urging his attention back to them, but he gazed instead at Abby.

'I'm so sorry.' Despite the distance, Abby could clearly hear his whispered words. 'I gave you time to try to find them. I can spare no more, or countless other mothers will weep for their children – mothers still living, and mothers in the spirit world.'

Abby cried out in an anguished wail as he turned back to the ensorcellment. The two women tried to comfort her, but Abby was not to be comforted in her grief.

Thunder rolled through the hills. A clacking clamour from the spell around Zedd rose to echo up and down the valley. Shafts of intense light shot upward. It was a disorienting sight, light shining up into sunlight.

Across the river, the counter to Zedd's magic seemed to spring forth. Arms of light twisted like smoke, lowering to tangle with the light radiating up around Zedd. The fog along the riverbank diffused suddenly.

In answer, Zedd spread his arms wide. The glowing, tumbling furnace of molten light thundered. The water sluicing over it roared as it boiled and steamed. The air wailed as if in protest.

Behind the wizard across the river, D'Haran soldiers poured out of the trees, driving their prisoners before them. People cried out in terror. They quailed at the wizard's magic, only to be driven onward by the spears and swords at their backs.

Abby saw several who refused to move fall to the blades. At the mortal cries, the rest rushed onward, like sheep before wolves.

If whatever Zedd was doing failed, the army of the Midlands would then charge into this valley to confront the enemy. The prisoners would be caught in the middle.

A figure working its way up along the opposite bank, dragging a child behind, caught Abby's attention. Her flesh flashed icy cold with sudden frigid sweat. It was Mariska. Abby shot a quick glance back over her shoulder. It was impossible. She squinted across the river.

'Nooo!' Zedd called out.

It was Zedd's little girl that Mariska had by the hair.

Somehow, Mariska had followed and found the child sleeping in Abby's home. With no one there to watch over her as she slept, Mariska had stolen the child back.

Mariska held the child out before herself, for Zedd to see. 'Cease and surrender, Zorander, or she dies!'

Abby tore away from the arms holding her and charged into the water. She struggled to run against the current, to reach the wizard. Part way there, he turned to stare into her eyes.

Abby froze. 'I'm sorry.' Her own voice sounded to her like a plea before death. 'I thought she was safe.'

Zedd nodded in resignation. It was out of his hands. He turned back to the enemy. His arms lifted to his sides. His fingers spread, as if commanding all to stop – magic and men alike.

'Let the prisoners go!' Zedd called across the water to the enemy wizard. 'Let them go, Anargo, and I'll give you all your lives!'

Anargo's laugh rang out over the water.

'Surrender,' Mariska hissed, 'or she dies.'

The old woman pulled out the knife she kept in the wrap around her waist. She pressed the blade to the child's throat. The girl was screaming in terror, her arms reaching to her father, her little fingers clawing the air.

Abby struggled ahead into the water. She called out, begging Mariska to let Zedd's daughter go free. The woman paid no more heed to Abby than to Zedd.

'Last chance!' Mariska called.

'You heard her,' Anargo growled out across the water. 'Surrender now or she will die.'

'You know I can't put myself above my people!' Zedd called back. 'This is between us, Anargo! Let them all go!'

Anargo's laugh echoed up and down the river. 'You are a fool, Zorander! You had your choice!' His expression twisted to rage. 'Kill her!' He screamed to Mariska.

Fists at his side, Zedd shrieked. The sound seemed to split the morning with its fury.

Mariska lifted the squealing child by her hair. Abby gasped in disbelief as the woman sliced the little girl's throat.

The child flailed. Blood spurted across Mariska's gnarly fingers as she viciously sawed the blade back and forth. She gave a final, mighty yank of the knife. The blood-soaked body dropped in a limp heap. Abby felt vomit welling up in the back of her throat. The silty dirt of the riverbank turned a wet red.

Mariska held the severed head high with a howl of victory. Strings of flesh and blood swung beneath it. The mouth hung in a slack, silent cry.

Abby threw her arms around Zedd's legs. 'Dear spirits, I'm sorry! Oh, Zedd, forgive me!'

She wailed in anguish, unable to gather her senses at witnessing a sight so grisly.

'And now, child,' Zedd asked in a hoarse voice from above, 'what would you have me do? Would you have me let them win, to save your daughter from what they have done to mine? Tell me, child, what should I do?'

Abby couldn't beg for the life of her family at a cost of such people rampaging unchecked across the land. Her sickened heart wouldn't allow it. How could she sacrifice the lives and peace of everyone else just so her loved ones would live?

She would be no better than Mariska, killing innocent children.

'Kill them all!' Abby screamed up at the wizard. She threw her arm out, pointing at Mariska and the hateful wizard Anargo. 'Kill the bastards! Kill them all!'

As if in obedience to her command, Zedd's arms flung upward. The morning cracked with a peal of thunder. The molten mass before him plunged into the water. The ground shook with a jolt. A huge geyser of water exploded forth. The air itself quaked. All around the most dreadful rumbling whipped the water into froth.

Abby, squatted down with the water to her waist, felt numb not only from the cold, but also from the cold knowledge that she'd been forsaken by the good spirits she had always thought would watch over her. Zedd turned and snatched her arm, dragging her up on the rock with him.

It was another world.

The shapes around them called to her, too. They reached out, bridging the distance between life and death. Searing pain, frightful joy, profound peace, spread through her at their touch. Light moved up through her body, filling her like air filled her lungs, and exploded in showers of sparks in her mind's eye. The thick howl of the magic was deafening.

Green light ripped through the water. Across the river, Anargo had been thrown to the ground. The rock atop which he had stood had shattered into needle-like shards. The soldiers called out in fright as the air all about danced with swirling smoke and sparks of light.

'Run!' Mariska screamed. 'While you have the chance!

Run for your lives!' Already she was racing towards the hills. 'Leave the prisoners to die! Save yourselves! Run!'

The mood across the river suddenly galvanized with a single determination. The D'Harans dropped their weapons. They cast aside the ropes and chains holding the prisoners, turned, and ran. In a single instant, the whole of an army that had a moment before stood grimly facing them, were all, as if of a single fright, running for their lives.

From the corner of her eye, Abby saw the Mother Confessor and the sorceress struggling to run into the water. Although the water was hardly above their knees, it bogged them down in their rush nearly as much as would mud.

Abby watched it all as if in a dream. She floated in the light surrounding her. Pain and rapture were one within her. Light and dark, sound and silence, joy and sorrow, all were one, everything and nothing together in a cauldron of howling, raging magic.

Across the river, the D'Haran army had vanished into the woods. Dust rose above the trees, marking their horses, wagons, and footfalls racing away, while at the riverbank, the Mother Confessor and the sorceress were shoving people into the water, screaming at them, though Abby didn't hear the words, so absorbed was she by the strange harmonious trills twisting her thoughts into visions of dancing colour overlaying what her eyes were trying to tell her.

She thought briefly that surely she was dying. She thought briefly that it didn't matter. And then her mind was swimming again in the cold colour and hot light, the drumming music of magic and worlds meshing. The wizard's embrace made her feel as if she were being held in her mother's arms again. Maybe she was.

Abby was aware of the people reaching the Midlands side of the river and running ahead of the Mother Confessor and sorceress. They vanished into the rushes and then Abby saw them far away, beyond the tall grass, running uphill, away from the sublime sorcery erupting from the river.

The world thundered around her. A subterranean thump brought sharp pain deep in her chest. A whine, like steel being shredded, tore through the morning air. All around the water danced and quaked.

Hot steam felt as if it would scald Abby's legs. The air went white with it. The noise hurt her ears so much that she squeezed her eyes shut. She saw the same thing with her eyes closed as she saw with them open – shadowy shapes swirling through the green air. Everything was going crazy in her mind, making no sense. Green fury tore at her body and soul.

Abby felt pain, as if something inside her tore asunder. She gasped and opened her eyes. A horrific wall of green fire was receding away from them, towards the far side of the river. Founts of water lashed upward, like a thuderstorm in reverse. Lightning laced together above the surface of the river.

As the conflagration reached the far bank, the ground beneath it rent apart. Shafts of violet light shot up from the ripping wounds in the earth, like the blood of another realm.

Worse, though, than any of it, were the howls. Howls of the dead, Abby was sure. It felt as if her own soul moaned in sympathy with the agony of cries filling the air.

From the receding green wall of glimmering fire, the shapes twisted and turned, calling, begging, trying to escape the world of the dead.

She understood now that that was what the wall of green fire was – death, come to life.

The wizard had breached the boundary between worlds.

Abby had no idea how much time passed; in the grip of the strange light in which she swam there seemed to be no time, any more than there was anything solid. There was nothing familiar about any of the sensations upon which to hang understanding.

It seemed to Abby that the wall of green fire had halted its advance in the trees on the far hillside. The trees over which it had passed, and those she could see embraced by the shimmering curtain, had blackened and shrivelled at the profound touch of death itself. Even the grass over which the grim presence had passed looked to have been baked black and crisp by a high summer sun.

As Abby watched the wall, it dulled. As she stared, it seemed to waver in and out of her vision, sometimes a glimmering green gloss, like molten glass, and sometimes no more than a pale hint, like a fog just now passed from the air.

To each side, it was spreading, a wall of death raging across the world of life.

Abby realized she heard the river again, the comfortable, common, sloshing, lapping, burbling sounds that she lived her life hearing but most of the time didn't notice.

Zedd hopped down from the rock. He took her hand and helped her down. Abby gripped his hand tightly to brace against the dizzying sensations swimming through her head.

Zedd snapped his fingers, and the rock upon which they had just stood leaped into the air, causing her to gasp in fright. In an instant so brief that she doubted she had seen it, Zedd caught the rock. It had become a small stone, smaller than an egg. He winked at her as he slipped it into a pocket. She thought the wink the oddest thing she could imagine, odder even than the boulder, now a stone in his pocket.

On the riverbank, the Mother Confessor and the sorceress waited. When Abby reached them, they took her arms, helping her out of the water first, and then Zedd.

The sorceress looked grim. 'Zedd, why isn't it moving?'

It sounded to Abby more like an accusation than a question. Either way, Zedd ignored it.

'Zedd,' Abby said in a painful undertone, 'I'm so sorry. It's my fault. I shouldn't have left her alone. I should have stayed. I'm so sorry.'

The wizard, seeming hardly to hear her words, was watching the wall of death on the other side of the river. He brought his clawed fingers up past his chest, appearing to call forth some inward resolve. Teeth clenched, his face set in a grim look of focused concentration.

With a sudden thump to the air, fire erupted between his hands. He held it out as he would hold an offering. Abby, along with the other two women, threw an arm up to protect her face from the heat.

Zedd lifted the roiling ball of liquid fire. It grew between his hands, tumbling and turning, roaring and hissing with rage.

The three women staggered back from the incandescent wrath. Abby had heard of such fire. She had once heard her mother name it in a hushed tone: wizard's fire. Even then, not seeing or knowing its like, those whispered words forming a picture in Abby's mind as her mother recounted it, had sent a chill through Abby. Wizard's fire was the bane of life, called forth to scourge an enemy. This could be nothing else.

'For killing my love, my Erilyn, the mother of our daughter, and all the other innocent loved ones of innocent people,' Zedd whispered, 'I send you, Panis Rahl, the gift of death.'

The wizard opened his arms outward. The liquid blue and yellow fire, bidden by its master, tumbled forward, gathering speed, roaring away towards D'Hara. As it crossed the river, it grew like angry lightning blooming forth, wailing with wrathful fury, reflecting in glimmering points from the water in thousands of bright sparkles.

The wizard's fire shot across the growing wall of green, just catching the upper edge. At the contact, green flame flared forth, some of it tearing away, caught up behind the wizard's fire, trailing after like smoke behind flame. The deadly mix howled off towards the horizon. Everyone stood transfixed, watching, until all trace of it had vanished in the distance.

When Zedd, pale and drawn, turned back to them, Abby clutched his robes. 'Zedd, I'm so sorry. I shouldn't—'

He put his fingers to her lips to silence her. 'There is someone waiting for you.'

He tilted his head. She turned. Back by the rushes, Philip stood holding Jana's hand. Abby gasped with a jolt of giddy joy. Philip grinned his familiar grin. At his other side, her father smiled and nodded his approval to her.

Arms reaching, Abby ran to them. Jana's face wrinkled. She backed against her father. Abby fell to her knees before her daughter.

'It's Mama,' Philip said to Jana. 'She just has herself some new clothes.'

Abby thought Jana was simply frightened by the red leather outfit, but she realized, then, where her daughter was staring. Abby grinned through her tears as she pulled free the long braid and tossed it away.

'Mama!' Jana cried at seeing the smile.

Abby threw her arms around her daughter. She laughed and hugged Jana so hard the child squeaked in protest. Abby felt Philip's hand on her shoulder in loving greeting. Abby stood and threw an arm around him, tears choking her voice. Her father put a comforting hand to her back while she squeezed Jana's hand.

Zedd, Delora, and the Mother Confessor herded them up the hill towards the people waiting at the top. Soldiers, mostly officers, some that Abby recognized, a few other people from Aydindril, and the wizard Thomas waited with the freed prisoners. Among the people liberated were those of Coney Crossing; people who held Abby, the daughter of a sorceress, in no favour. But they were her people, the people from her home, the people she had wanted saved.

Zedd rested a hand on Abby's shoulder. Abby was shocked to see that his wavy brown hair was now partly snow-white. She knew without a looking-glass that hers had undergone the same transformation in the place beyond the world of life, where, for a time, they had been.

'This is Abigail, born of Helsa,' the wizard called out to the people gathered. 'She is the one who went to Aydindril to seek my help. Though she does not have magic, it is because of her that you people are all free. She cared enough to beg for your lives.'

Abby, with Philip's arm around her waist and Jana's hand in hers, looked from the wizard to the sorceress, and then to the Mother Confessor. The Mother Confessor smiled. Abby thought it a cold-hearted thing to do in view of the fact that Zedd's daughter had been murdered before their eyes not long before. She whispered as much.

The Mother Confessor's smile widened. 'Don't you remember?' she asked as she leaned close. 'Don't you remember what I told you we call him?'

Abby, confused by everything that had happened, couldn't imagine what the Mother Confessor was talking about. When she admitted she didn't, the Mother Confessor and the sorceress shepherded her onward, past the grave where Abby had reburied her mother's skull upon her return, and into the house.

Standing to the side, out of the way, the Mother Confessor eased back the door to Abby's bedroom. Abby stared in disbelief. There, snug in the bed where Abby had placed her, in the bed from where Mariska had stolen her, was Zedd's daughter, still sleeping peacefully.

'The trickster,' the Mother Confessor said. 'I told you that was our name for him.'

'And not a very flattering one,' Zedd grumbled as he stepped up behind them.

'But . . . how?' Abby pressed her fingers to her temples. 'I don't understand.'

Zedd gestured. Abby saw, for the first time, the body lying just beyond the door out the back. It was Mariska.

'When you showed me the room when we first came here,' Zedd told her, 'I laid a few traps for those intent on harm. That woman was killed by those traps because she came here intent on taking my daughter from where she slept.'

'You mean it was all an illusion?' Abby was dumb-founded. 'Why would you do such a cruel thing? How could you?'

'I am the object of vengeance,' the wizard explained. 'I didn't want my daughter to pay the price her mother has already paid. Since my spell killed the woman as she tried to harm my daughter, I was able to use a vision of her to accomplish the deception. The enemy knew the woman, and that she acted for Anargo. I used what they expected to see to convince them and to frighten them into running and leaving the prisoners.

'I cast the death spell so that everyone would think they saw my daughter being killed. I did it to protect her from the unforeseen. This way, the enemy thinks my daughter dead, and will have no reason to hunt her or ever again try to harm her.'

The sorceress scowled at him. 'If it were any but you, Zeddicus, and for any reason but the reason you had, I'd see you brought up on charges for casting such a web as a death spell.' She broke into a grin. 'Well done, First Wizard.'

Outside, the officers all wanted to know what was happening.

'No battle today,' Zedd called out to them. 'I've just ended the war.'

They cheered with genuine joy. Had Zedd not been the First Wizard, Abby suspected they would have hoisted him on their shoulders. It seemed that there was no one more glad for peace than those whose job it was to fight for it.

Wizard Thomas, looking more humble than Abby had ever seen him, cleared his throat. 'Zorander, I . . . I . . . I simply can't believe what my own eyes have seen.' His face finally took on its familiar scowl. 'But we have people already in near revolt over magic. When news of this spreads, it is only going to make it worse. The demands for relief from magic grow every day and you have fed the fury. With this, we're liable to have revolt on our hands.'

'I still want to know why it isn't moving,' Delora growled from behind. 'I want to know why it's just sitting there, all green and still.'

Zedd ignored her and directed his attention to the old wizard. 'Thomas, I have a job for you.'

He motioned several officers and officials from Aydindril forward, and passed a finger before all their faces, his own turning grim and determined. 'I have a job for all of you. The people have reason to fear magic. Today we have seen magic deadly and dangerous. I can understand why they fear it.

'In appreciation of these fears, I shall grant their wish.'

'What!' Thomas scoffed. 'You can't end magic, Zorander! Not even you can accomplish such a paradox.'

'Not end it,' Zedd said. 'But give them a place without it. I want you to organize an official delegation large enough to travel all the Midlands with the offer. All those who would quit a world with magic are to move to the lands to the west. There they shall set up new lives free of any magic. I shall ensure that magic cannot intrude on their peace.'

Thomas threw up his hands. 'How can you make such a promise?'

Zedd's arm lifted to point off behind him, to the wall of green fire growing towards the sky. 'I shall call up a second wall of death, through which none can pass. On the other side it shall be a place free of magic. There, people will be free to live their lives without magic.

'I want you all to see that the word is passed through the land. People have until spring to emigrate to the lands west. Thomas, you will warrant that none with magic make the journey. We have books we can use to ensure that we purge a place of any with a trace of magic. We can assure that there will be no magic there.

'In the spring, when all who wish have gone to their new homeland, I will seal them off from magic. In one fell swoop, I will satisfy the large majority of the petitions that come to us; they will have lives without magic. May the good spirits watch over them, and may they not come to regret their wish granted.'

Thomas pointed heatedly at the thing Zedd had brought into the world. 'But what about that thing? What if people go wandering into it in the dark? They will be walking into death.'

'Not only in the dark,' Zedd said. 'Once it has stabilized it will be hard to see at all. We will have to set up guards to keep people away. We will have to set aside land near the boundary and have men guard the area to keep people out.'

'Men?' Abby asked. 'You mean you will have to start a corps of boundary wardens?'

'Yes,' Zedd said, his eyebrows lifting, 'that's a good name for them. Boundary wardens.'

Silence settled over those leaning in to hear the wizard's words. The mood had changed and was now serious with the grim matter at hand. Abby couldn't imagine a place without magic, but she knew how vehemently some wished it.

Thomas finally nodded. 'Zedd, this time I think you've got it right. Sometimes, we must serve the people by not serving them.' The others mumbled their agreement, though, like Abby, it seemed to them a bleak solution.

Zedd straightened. 'Then it is decided.'

He turned and announced to the crowd the end of the war, and the division to come in which those who had petitioned for years would finally have their petition granted; for those who wished it, a land outside the Midlands, without magic, would be created.

While everyone was chattering about such a mysterious and exotic thing as a land without magic, or cheering and celebrating the end of the war, Abby whispered to Jana to wait with her father a moment. She kissed her daughter and then took the opportunity to pull Zedd aside.

'Zedd, may I speak with you? I have a question.'

Zedd smiled and took her by the elbow, urging Abby into her small home. 'I'd like to check on my daughter. Come along.'

Abby cast caution to the winds and took the Mother Confessor's hand in one of hers, Delora's in the other, and pulled them in with her. They had a right to hear this, too.

'Zedd,' Abby asked once they were away from the

crowd in her yard, 'may I please know the debt your father owed my mother?'

Zedd lifted an eyebrow. 'My father owed your mother no debt.'

Abby was overcome with a bewildered frown. 'But it was a debt of bones, passed down from your father to you, and from my mother to me.'

'Oh, it was a debt all right, but not owed to your mother, but by your mother.'

'What?' Abby asked in stunned confusion. 'What do you mean?'

Zedd smiled. 'When your mother was giving birth to you, she was in trouble. You both were dying in the labour. My father used magic to save her. Helsa begged him to save you, too. In order to keep you in the world of the living and out of the Keeper's grasp, without thought to his own safety, he worked far beyond the endurance anyone would expect of a wizard.

'Your mother was a sorceress, and understood the extent of what was involved in saving your life. She recognized full well the personal risk he took. In appreciation of what my father had done, she swore a debt to him. When she died, the debt passed to you.'

Abby, eyes wide, tried to reconcile the whole thing in her mind. Her mother had never told her the nature of the debt.

'But . . . but you mean that it is I who owe the debt to you? You mean that the debt of bones is my burden?'

Zedd pushed open the door to the room where his daughter slept, smiling as he looked in. 'The debt is paid, Abby. The bracelet your mother gave you had magic, linking you to the debt. Thank you for my daughter's life.'

Abby glanced to the Mother Confessor. Trickster indeed. 'But why would you help me, if it was really not a debt of bones you owed me? If it was really a debt I owed you?'

Zedd shrugged. 'We reap a reward merely in the act of helping others. We never know how, or if, that reward will come back to us. Helping is the reward; none other is needed nor better.'

Abby watched the beautiful little girl sleeping in the room beyond. 'I am thankful to the good spirits that I could help keep such a life in this world. I may not have the gift, but I can foresee that she will go on to be a person of import, not only for you, but for others.'

Zedd smiled idly as he watched his daughter sleeping. 'I think you may have the gift of prophecy, my dear, for she is already a person who has played a part in bringing a war to an end, and in so doing, saved the lives of countless people.'

The sorceress pointed heatedly out the window. 'I still want to know why that thing isn't moving. It was supposed to pass over D'Hara and purge it of all life, to kill them all for what they have done.' Her scowl deepened. 'Why is it just sitting there?'

Zedd folded his hands. 'It ended the war. That is enough. The wall is a part of the underworld itself, the world of the dead. Their army will not be able to cross it and make war on us for as long as such a boundary stands.'

'And how long will that be?'

Zedd shrugged. 'Nothing remains for ever. For now, there will be peace. The killing is ended.'

The sorceress did not look to be satisfied. 'But they were trying to kill us all!'

'Well, now they can't. Delora, there are those in D'Hara who are innocent, too. Just because Panis Rahl wished to conquer and subjugate us, that does not mean that all the D'Haran people are evil. Many good people in D'Hara have suffered under harsh rule. How could I kill everyone there, including all the people who have caused no harm, and themselves wish only to live their lives in peace?'

Delora wiped a hand across her face. 'Zeddicus, sometimes I don't know about you. Sometimes, you make a lousy wind of death.'

The Mother Confessor stood staring out the window, towards D'Hara. Her violet eyes turned back to the wizard.

'There will be those over there who will be your foes for life because of this, Zedd. You have made bitter enemies with this. You have left them alive.'

'Enemies,' the wizard said, 'are the price of honour.'